HOW NOT TO TALK LIKE AN ARSE

101 WORDS YOU SHOULDN'T USE ANY TIME SOON

RICHARD WILSON

PORTICO

'Do not be so open-minded that your brains fall out.'
G.K. Chesterton

Published in the United Kingdom in 2011 by
Portico Books
10 Southcombe Street
London
W14 0RA

An imprint of Anova Books Company Ltd

ISBN 978-19075-542-0-9

A CIP catalogue record for this book is available from the British Library.

10 9 8 7 6 5 4 3 2 1

Printed and bound by CPI Mackays, Chatham ME5 8TD

This book can be ordered direct from the publisher at www.anovabooks.com

Thank you for buying **HOW NOT TO TALK LIKE AN ARSE**. We hope you enjoy reading Richard Wilson's book as much as we enjoyed putting it together. Having said that we didn't enjoy it quite as much as the Snooker which was on the television quite a lot of the time and really quite distracting. So rather than talking like arses we ended up printing like arses. We would therefore like to apologise for the following errors:

••

Inside Flap: errant apostrophe in 'Richard Wilson's'

P. 26 top line missing: 'for their country?
OK – if you're still with me – Tears for Fears …'

P. 29 top line missing: ''confess' something,
the implication is that you've done …'

P. 106 last line missing: 'country; they also play
Eton Fives but we don't all go on about the 'top step',
do we? Football dwarfs all other sports in terms of …'

PP. 28 and 169 where line repetition occurs

••

Enjoy the book.

Portico Books

Contents

● ●

Introduction

● ●

'Hey! Do the math; I'm your go-to guy 24/7.
Going forward, just chillax. It's a no-brainer. End of.'

Someone somewhere near you has probably just uttered a
sentence like that. Just as in most big cities you are never more
than six feet from a rat, you are also probably only seconds away
from an offensive ejaculation like 'OMG! That's literally genius!'

Who or what is to blame for this outbreak of idiocy? I could
point the finger across the Atlantic, where many of the words
and phrases that can really make a grown man flinch originate.
American celebrity culture in general, and those terrible trollops
from *Sex and the City* in particular, must shoulder a heavy burden
of guilt for popularising the vocabulary of conspicuous
consumption and celebrity obsession. With their 'inner divas',
'must-haves', 'frenemies' and 'Brangelinas' they influenced a
generation of our own useless, lazy journalists on style
supplements and property-porn mags, not to mention all those
who watch too many 'seasons' of American TV series and
squeal 'Don't go there, girlfriend' at each other in homage.

There is also the pernicious influence of the corporate world,
with its ludicrous self-styled Alpha Male/sports-jock culture,
which has generated its own particularly foul-smelling sample of
bullshit. I'm not just talking about business jargon here; many

have already vented their spleen over the ridiculousness of 'negative value drivers', 'disability outreach workers' and 'waste management solutions'. That kind of language is designed to take the colour *out* of life, to make interesting things or controversial statements boring, but many of the words and phrases in this book are risible and despicable because the people who use them think they give the boring aspects of their own life substantially more *wow* factor.

Of course the English language evolves. That, as I'm sure someone will tell me, is a no-brainer. But I'm not against slang; I use it all the time. I would never under any circumstances say 'I'm loving' slang, but it certainly does add to the richness and variety of life. Kids will always invent new words to confuse and annoy grown-ups – 'phatt', 'sick', 'blud' – they could be from Nigel Molesworth's exercise book for all I know and they probably mean the exact opposite now to what they did a couple of years ago (maybe this year, 'sick' does actually mean 'unwell'). But some slang sticks. I have no problem with 'telly', 'fridge', 'cash' or 'mate' – they have become an acceptable part of the English language, and who would deny young people their bit of fun with words? We should encourage and patronise them whenever possible.

But most of the words and phrases in this book have nothing to do with the evolution of language and *everything* to do with fad and fashion and making older people (who should know better than to bother with such things) feel like they are 'on trend' and 'in the loop'. I'm not advocating an *Eats, Shoots and Leaves* attitude to words and phrases; my gripe with these sayings is not a class/sex/race thing. Grammar and punctuation pedantry lead you inevitably to snobbishness but it's not about education or lack of it; it's about lapses of taste and judgement. John Humphrys or Evan Davis on the *Today* programme are now just as likely to say 'End of' as a hairdresser in Chigwell.

Most academic linguists are reluctant to pass judgement on particular developments in language. They are descriptive rather than prescriptive, and some take great delight in progress of any kind. Before I began writing this book I consulted the eminent linguist Professor David Crystal. He had been a very entertaining guest on a TV programme I had made about texting language and I sought his advice about writing this book. He said:

There are too many books of that kind around already. I don't think there's anything to be gained by having one person's irritations thrust down other people's mouths, especially when they fly in the face of general usage.

Oh well. Sorry, Professor, I'll admit this book is not a considered linguistic appraisal of developments in modern language. It *is* about my irritations, though I don't believe they are exclusive to me. But it's also about taking the moral high ground: the words and phrases in this book do have a kind of immorality about them because they are fake, false, dishonest and encourage the user to pretend to be something they are not.

Businessmen use the language of sport to make sitting at a desk and 'pinging' emails to each other seem heroic; sportsmen use the language of business to give the impression they are following some carefully thought-out plan as they clatter into each other. British people who should be proud of their innate dullness try to make out that they are in a series finale of an American TV drama; people in IT talk as if they were launching a mission to Neptune, and there are thousands of people in all walks of life abducting innocent nouns and forcing them to be verbs. It's technically known as *anthimeria*, which sounds like a cross between an infectious disease and an illegal practice and it should be avoided as much as either.

As proof that the propensity to talk like an arse is spreading to the most unlikely quarters, my wife received an email recently from a local pub, which is trying to attract more women at lunchtime. It's in an area with plenty of stay-at-home mothers, so she might have expected the level of arse-speak to be quite high ('carbs', 'high-end', 'to die for' etc) but nothing could have prepared her for this:

Introducing the 'Mummy Me Time' Club

Whether you consider yourself more 'slummy' than 'yummy',
every mummy needs some quality 'me time'.

After rubbing her eyes and doing a Tom and Jerry-esque double take, she realised the bar was hosting a convivial hints and tips session for mothers on simple DIY and household wisdom. It concluded:

After the lesson, kick back with the girls and enjoy a
well-earned glass of wine.
'Mummy Me Time' – for those trying to live the dream,
love life and have a giggle in between.

It's hard to believe that the author of this email could cram so many offensive words and phrases into just a few short paragraphs but there they are. And yet, though I take my hat off to the Mummy Me Time Club they are still a long way off being the worst offenders. That honour belongs indisputably to the contestants on *The Apprentice*; aspiring big-shot graduates who will happily cluster-bomb their conversations with Americanisms and every known variety of arse-speak because they are a) trying to impress b) in 'business' c) on television and d) want to be quoted in the press. It's hard to imagine a more toxic combination of personal attributes and it's no wonder millions tune in to see them humiliated.

Every person working in an office who watches *The Apprentice* has surely had the same thought – 'I hope to God I'm not like that'. But I'm afraid, if nothing is done to fight the epidemic, you, dear reader, could wake up one day and find that, like Donald Sutherland in *The Invasion of the Bodysnatchers*, you are the only person left who is not talking like a complete arse. So we'll just have to start correcting or, better still, mocking each other.

Don't underestimate the power of ridicule. Cast your mind all the way back to the early years of the 21st century when the Post Office became *Consignia*. This was around the time when dozens of filthy-rich companies were blowing millions on image consultants to change their names to nonsense like *Unisys* and *Accenture* and *Monday*. Everyone could see that *Consignia* was a) stupid, b) nothing to do with posting letters and c) not even a proper word and, amid a barrage of derision from the public and business bigwigs, it was consignia-ed to the dustbin of history and replaced with the slightly more obvious Royal Mail.

So small victories can be achieved through simple, straightforward derision. It's going to be awkward and possibly embarrassing. If you have friends who talk like arses, you may be forced to lose some. If they're the sort of people who can't see the problem, you might be better off without them. So start by having a read of this list. (It was going to be arranged into various categories representing different walks of life but it soon became obvious that, like some sinister strain of bird flu, arse-speak can jump from one to another.) Then prepare yourself for action. When someone mentions J-Lo, ask 'Is that her *real* name?' When another says 'Any time soon', say 'Do you mean "in the near future"?' When someone says 'You're really working that look' say 'Do you mean that you like my clothes?' If a person uses '24/7' and 'You do the math' in the same sentence, just reply with 3.42857143. And if anyone says 'Go figure', I'm afraid you'll just have to kill them.

Where do stupid words come from?

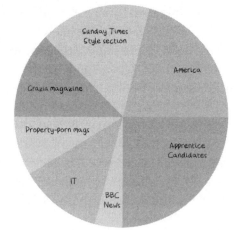

Trending

● ●

Twitter has ushered in some genuinely horrible words, including the term, once innocently associated with birdsong, for an individual Twitter message, which I can't bring myself to write down.

Its phenomenal success also introduced us to the term 'microblogging' and allowed similar stupidly named 'microblogs' to surface such as Plurk, Jaiku, Pownce and Yodlr. Actually I've made that last one up, although you can buy yodlr.com and I'm sure sooner or later someone will create a social networking service through which people can communicate with each other only in high-pitched Swiss-German.

'Trending' is one of Twitter's greater crimes. If something is 'trending' on Twitter, it means a lot of people on Twitter are referring to that same thing. Now, although the very mention of Twitter is enough to send many right-thinking people into spasm, it has to be said of the thing itself that, like a lot of modern phenomena, it's not nearly as bad as I thought it was going to be. The internet, mobile phones, the Dyson Airblade, Graham Norton – they have all surprised me with their utility, convenience and decent jokes. In the same way, Twitter has its plus points. It's not intrusive – it takes quite a lot of effort to enter the space where Twittering is done, so, if you can dodge those newspapers that like to fill their columns with the brief ramblings of narcissists, it's easy to avoid. And the 140-character limit stops people rabbiting on for too long (unless you are someone like Richard Herring who seems to be at it all day) and at least while they are twittering they are not talking to you.

The trouble with 'trending' is that it's in danger of gaining currency among normal people. I may have already missed Robert Peston or Stephanie Flanders telling the BBC News audience that 'the economy is trending downwards', but it's only a matter of time before they're all at it. 'Sunny intervals in the morning, cloudy later trending rainy.' 'After the Lib Dems lose another by-election, Nick Clegg is trending suicidal.' 'Another defeat for Chelsea. They're trending relegation.' No matter how appealing some of those headlines seem, we really can't allow this to happen. If you want to join my group of like-minded Luddites, sign in at www.yodlr.com where you can *werden sie ein mitglied, und unsere erste sitzung ist nächste woche-odle ey hee heeeeeee!*

OMG!

● ●

It's only ever said as a joke, surely? But no, beyond the text language and the ironic use, there is a generation of people reaching adulthood – some are already there – who will drop *OMG!* in conversation as casually as a yes, no or maybe and with all. the. full stops. And the exclamation mark is obligatory, whether it's spoken or written.

Linguists, with their relentlessly positive attitude about the changes in our language, will claim that we humans have always enjoyed abbreviating language; acronyms like TTFN, SWALK, NORWICH and SNAFU have been around since the war years and often long before that.

The difference is that the technology and media did not exist to shove them in our faces 24 hours a day.

Further evidence of mankind's descent into the cultural abyss is the magazine *OMG,* which serves up celebrity and lifestyle gossip to the gay community (how gay is *that?*) and the website *omg!* (brought to you by Yahoo!). Take a look at this headline from a random trawl: 'OMG! Will Li-Lo face charges over alleged theft?' In my most paranoid and egotistic moments, I think they have designed this website specifically to infuriate me. Here's another one: 'OMG! Ashley Tisdale Debuts Her

New Nose!' I feel like the snowplough driver in *Gremlins* who can't quite believe that the little critters are about to run him down with his *own* vehicle – his worst nightmare coming true before his very eyes.

And still they come!

Gossip Girl is an extremely popular American TV show putting in a serious claim to be the worst television programme of all time (*Sex in the City* and *Mistresses* take some beating). It's about some teenage airheads whose lives feature in a blog written by a teenage airhead and the viewers are all teenage airheads. The show's catchphrase and theme song appears to be 'OMG!' and the promotional material – trailers/posters, etc. – all carry the letters 'OMG' and the internet is full of 'Top Five Gossip Girl OMG! Moments'.

It's easy to blame the Americans for the cluster-bombing of Western civilisation with excrement, but let no one forget that it was a British television producer who detonated *OMG! With Peaches Geldof* among crowds of defenceless viewers. It's a veritable neutron bomb of a show and our only hope is to dig a lead-lined bunker 50 feet underground until the toxic fallout has dispersed or someone at ITV2 cancels it.

Chillax

●●

Many of the words in this book will share the same construction as 'chillax' – a fusion of two fairly innocent words to make a new horrible one; in this case, one that sounds like something you'd buy in Boots to cure constipation.

What may have started as an ironic, jokey jumbling of 'chill out' and 'relax' is now in danger of passing into everyday language, thanks mainly to the ease with which a whole panoply of products and services can be gathered under its umbrella. Record labels, masseurs, acupuncturists, travel agents and, weirdly, a worldwide chain of hookah pipe restaurants are all currently urging us to 'chillax' with their wares.

The growth of the relaxation industry baffles me. We are probably the least physically and mentally challenged of any generation in history. Every task from washing clothes to long division is made easier by machines whose technological advances are outstripping our ability to imagine them. Music, TV, films, games and books are all cheaper and easier to access than they've ever been. Keeping in touch with one another across thousands of miles is just like talking to a person in the same room. A teenager today can't even begin to understand the frustration of queuing up outside a piss-drenched public telephone box with a handful of ten-pence pieces for about five minutes of conversation with a girl in Nottingham.

I'm not one for relaxing myself; nothing could make me more tense than a massage and my natural reaction to being told to chill out or relax is to dig my nails into my hands and bristle. What is doubly or even triply annoying about the word is that it is never used in the first person. No one ever says 'I've done a hard day's work, I'm going to chillax'; they only ever throw it back at someone else as an order – usually their parents or an older, wiser, superior being (i.e. me) who is trying to get them to do some work, generally smarten themselves up and take off whatever stupid hat they happen to be wearing indoors. Like its evil cousins, 'take a chill pill' and 'loosen up', 'chillax' is an order from the New Age/hippy/slacker's rule book which must be resisted with every fibre of our being.

Heads-Up

● ●

At the time of writing, this hideous piece of business jargon is still to elbow its way into our everyday lives. I've yet to hear, for example, of anyone who gets first look at a restaurant bill saying, 'OK, guys, let me give you a heads-up. We're looking at £62.50 payable in four instalments. Spreading the risk around, I'd say we're talking ballpark sixteen quid each; with tip seventeen, tops.' Or a mother on Christmas Eve telling her excited children gathered around the fireplace – 'Heads up, everyone. We're expecting the gift-guy to rock up here any time post-midnight and he's totally across your 2011 behaviour history 24/7 so, if you haven't delivered, he won't deliver. Clear? OK, let's see some sleeping, people!'

'Heads-up' has its origins, like a lot of bollocks, in American sport and military slang. It's no real surprise that the two are connected – most of the gibberish you can hear from the players on a ballpark or a football field could easily echo around a military base in Afghanistan. 'Heads-up' is about keeping alert or focused. A basketball team will be praised for playing 'heads-up basketball'. This presumably means looking about you all the time, noticing what your team-mates and the opposition are doing so that you can ask yourself 'Why are my shorts so big?'

Or it's a warning or briefing to a group of people by someone in charge – an army officer to a group of lower ranks who rely on the superior officer for guidance, leadership, respect – that something significant is about to happen, i.e. he is going to talk bollocks for the next ten minutes.

This expression in turn may have given rise to the 'heads-up display' – a clever bit of military technology which projects instrument panels in front of a jet pilot's eyes so he doesn't have to look down. It gives him vital information on airspeed, target location and altitude, so he can drop his bombs with precision onto the Afghan wedding party. Politicians and businessmen adapted the technology so they could talk straight at the audience without appearing to read from carefully prepared bullshit on the lectern in front of them. It's known colloquially as the 'sincerity machine', which tells you all you need to know about phrases like this.

However appropriate 'heads-up' may be in the macho world of sport or modern warfare, the fact that certain people in perfectly safe and rather boring office jobs repeatedly use this phrase is just another indication of how far they will go to build their part up. What's worse is that more and more people are failing to see the ridiculousness of it all and joining in. That's when the exchange of tosh becomes two-way and some overly keen, overly ambitious jerk responds to a piece of vaguely useful information with 'thanks for the heads-up'. When shit begins to flow in two directions, it's time to borrow another phrase from the military – duck and cover.

Good to Go

• •

Ready. You don't need to say 'good to go', you can say 'ready'. You can say 'OK', you can say 'Right, that's everything sorted', you can say 'Go on, then', but with 'Good to go' you're probably trying to liven up your dull and tedious office life by pretending you're about to rescue Apollo 13. I imagine if you're 'good to go', you're also locked and loaded and, in all likelihood, totally pumped. Really, you've missed your vocation and you should have been at the head of Operation Desert Storm with Stormin' Norman Schwarzkopf.

I worked at a coal mine in the early 80s*, where the work was not glamorous but epic in a way that no job in Britain today could be described as such, and, when things were ready to be done or a button was to be pressed and heavy machinery was about to start moving, no one would ask, 'Are we good to go?' No. A massive bloke who could break you in half with one swipe of his snap tin would shout, 'WHAT'S THA FOOKIN DOOIN THEE? GERRARTON WAY THEZZA FOOKIN LORRY CUMMIN IN!'

---

*OK, as a wages clerk, but it was quite dirty.

But the phrase is rife in television and advertising circles, where the culture of hyperbole and overconfidence means that missions that are 'good to go' are nearly always doomed to failure.

Brains are stormed, ideas are sketched out, PowerPoint presentations are honed, jackets donned, cuffs shot, hair smoothed. The team leader looks around and says, 'We're in pretty good shape. We're good to go.' An hour later, they're back from the meeting with heads bowed, scowly faces and a list of excuses as long as your arm for why 'the idiots just didn't get it'. 'Good to go' is as deserving of failure as 'What could possibly go wrong?'

The eminent philosopher Roger Scruton (stay with me) recently wrote a terrific-sounding book called *The Uses of Pessimism and the Dangers of False Hope.* I haven't actually read it, but the title is inspiring enough on its own. Assuming things will just turn out well is not optimism, it is stupidity; the kind of stupidity that took Americans into Iraq, where they assumed everyone would embrace them as warmly as they would embrace democracy; Iraq, where I'm sure the phrase 'good to go' was said many times by young lads from Oklahoma just before they stepped on a roadside bomb. The upbeat, can-do attitude embedded in the phrase 'good to go' is exactly what everyone loves about the Americans but is the very thing which will ensure their eventual collapse as an economic power and enslavement by the Chinese.

Hurting

· ·

If you've never come across this term in a sugary US sitcom, such as *Friends* or *Glee*, or in a think-piece in *Grazia*, you might hear it every two years during a major international football tournament. 'Hurting' is the kind of word frequently used by football commentators after (yet another) abject performance by someone like Wayne Rooney or Frank Lampard in an England shirt. Actually, the biggest disappointment is usually Steven Gerrard – he slopes off the field like a lovesick hunchback while Guy Mowbray or Alan Shearer declares, 'He'll be hurting right now.' That's 'hurting right now' as opposed to feeling shame and embarrassment right now.

The players are happy to bandy the H-word around, too. At his first post-World Cup press conference in 2010, Gerrard mumbled under his breath, 'Obviously I'm hurting as a player.' What he meant to say was, 'Obviously I was useless as a player.' The objectively measurable fact of Gerrard and the rest of the England team's failure to live up to their salaries was turned around to focus on his 'feelings' about how shit he was.

And far from being outraged by successive England football captains sticking out the bottom lip at their misfortune, it seems people actively want their footballers to be soft and sensitive; to wax their scrotums and use moisturiser; to burst into tears after every defeat like Gazza. Many people indeed do credit the little fat Geordie's outburst at Italia 90 as the moment when real men were given permission to cry, but never was there a more misunderstood gesture. You could tell from Gazza's tomato-tinged face that he was suffering a childlike mixture of shame, rage and despair. There was nothing 'New Manly' about it. As Gary Lineker knew, Gazza had had a rush of blood to the head and somebody should've 'had a word with him'. That nobody ever did have a proper word with him is probably why the last we heard of Gazza was when he was trying to bring Raoul Moat a dressing gown and a chicken.

So, if Gazza wasn't to blame, how did the language of self-pity creep into the macho, spit-roasting, gang-raping, Audi-driving world of professional football? Well, stay with me on this …

Academic research* has discovered that the first usage of the word 'hurting', in the feeble intransitive sense, was coined in the early 80s by Curt Smith and Roland Orzabal, who as Tears for Fears released the slightly poor debut album of that name. The singles 'Mad World' and 'Pale Shelter' are two of the better tracks but the overall tone is set by the rather feeble 'Change' with what sounds like Patrick Moore playing xylophone.

Most 80s musicians would have been happy to brandish the use of a TV astronomer as a session musician as a sign of their avant-garde credentials but Curt and Roland decided to push the boundaries still further with their questionable use of the

*Made up.

24

word 'hurting' in the title track, and as perfectly illustrated on the front cover of the album by a blubbing child.

Now if the 'hurting' in question referred to the actual act of kicking this kid on the shins or throwing a stone at him, then I'm sure most people would have been fine with that. But no, the 'hurting' in question is emotional hurt, expressed by two of the most tonsorially challenged softies ever to walk the musical stage.

Emotional hurt used to be known as 'hurt feelings', which when you say it out loud does sound a bit pathetic and childish. And it's for precisely that reason that the therapy industry has put so much effort in the last 30 years into expanding the emotional vocabulary – to make our childish feelings seem more complex and 'grown up'.

Look at this extract from just one of the hundreds of Emotional Literacy websites:

Seems like most of this world only has two emotions: Rage and Apathy! Instead of the foundational emotions of Acceptance / Rejection, Control / Chaos, Security / Insecurity, Inclusion / Exclusion, Empathy / Non-Empathy and Sympathy / Unsympathetic. And surely there are more ways than this to describe ourselves?

Yes, I'm sure there is an almost infinite number of ways in which sadness, disappointment, shame or being a bit pissed off can be described to make people give us more attention and take us a bit more seriously. Isn't that great?

And what has all this got to do with self-pitying, beetle-browed Scousers bleating about not playing football very well ushered in a new brand of wimp-pop, closely followed by the even wimpier Lotus Eaters and China Crisis – both Liverpool bands who knocked about a bit with The Lightning Seeds, whose biggest hit was the Euro 96 anthem 'Three Lions' (lyrics by Frank Skinner and David Baddiel), with the chorus: 'Three Lions on a shirt, Jules Rimet still gleaming. Thirty years of *hurt* never stopped me dreaming.' How could the players on the pitch, not to mention little Stevie G at home in Huyton, with his cross of St George face-paint running down his wet cheeks like mascara, not be affected by it? I rest my case, m'lud.

Impact

● ●

I think we can all agree that the word 'impact' is a noun. It has been for quite a while and, to be fair to it, it's quite a good one as it's slightly onomatopoeic and is closely related to the rather excellent word 'impinge'.

'Impact' is a particularly useful word if you want to talk, for example, about the point at which a lethal comet will make contact with the Earth, leaving Bruce Willis to save the planet; or the effectiveness of Ole Gunnar Solskjaer's late introduction as a sub in the 1999 Champions League final, and it's an excellent choice of name for the most respected driving school in the whole of Acton, W12.

However, as a verb, 'impact' is shit. Its grammatical realignment began in mid-90s American corporate-speak and it now crops up among British politicians and policemen who want to appear, in their dealings with the media, totally up to speed with post-Blair jive-talk.

So you will have a Home Office minister defending 24-hour drinking with the phrase: 'We will have to see how this impacts crime statistics'. Oh, will we now? I might wait and see how this *affects* crime statistics – that seems reasonable enough; I might even wait and see what kind of impact this has *upon* crime statistics, but I am certainly not waiting for anything to 'impact' without even a preposition.

English is a fantastic language with a wonderfully wide range of different words to communicate the same thing; surely there's enough to satisfy the most desperately ambitious, attention-seeking show-off, without kidnapping some other words, meant for a *totally different* purpose, and grafting another meaning onto them, like an ear onto a mouse's back.

You can find a fair bit of internet discussion about whether or not it is permissible to use 'impact' as a verb. On one chatroom I found, a kid was upset that his English teacher had double-crossed out his use of the verb 'impact' and told the whole class never ever to use it as a verb again. I'd love to know who that teacher is so I could send him or her a fiver, but of course the web – and this chatroom in particular – is full of people who think 'your teacher is a total asshole'.

is full of people who think 'your teacher is a total asshole'. These people continue: 'Impact as a verb has become a thoroughly mainstream usage, and nobody should be penalised for using a construct that is used by the BBC and by quality newspapers such as *The Times* and the *Guardian*.'

To which I say – exactly. Exactly the point. The noun-as-verb menace is growing and people who should know better are doing nothing to stop it. Some really hideous ones like 'to podium', 'to medal' and 'to trend' are dealt with elsewhere in this book – but here are some other horrors to be going on with …

Fess Up

• •

This is supposed to be a shorter, cooler way of saying 'admit' or 'confess' but both of those words, like 'fess up', contain two syllables, so it doesn't save any time at all. It saves one letter. So it's an inappropriate and needlessly abbreviated way of doing something quite serious, like a judge wearing his wig at a jaunty angle while he's sentencing you to life imprisonment.

But there's another aspect to the use of 'fess up' that is even more annoying and, yes, downright dangerous. When you something seriously wrong, something you might even be ashamed of, but 'fess it up' and you've managed to trivialise it. Here's a revealing headline on MSN's web-thing:

'Why I Cheated' – Women Fess Up

So it's OK to 'fess up' to 'cheating'. No big deal. Whereas 'confessing' to infidelity sounds like you did a bad thing. This could and will catch on: fess up to a bit of embezzlement – 'I've so totally ripped you all off, it's embarrassing!' – or turn up to your local police station and 'fess up' to a number of brutal and ritualistic serial killings – 'Come on, guys, chillax! It's only murder.' Maybe you think I'm taking all this a bit too seriously, and it's good that the language has evolved so we can remove some of the guilt from our lives. Well, in my view, guilt is sadly underrated; it's one of the few things that separates us from the beasts, a natural in-built mechanism for steering clear of wrongdoing, but I'll happily dispense with it if we can institute a universally acceptable system of instant fines and punishment beatings for serious transgressions – such as the use of 'fess up'.

Learnings

● ●

This is the 21st-century tosser's way of saying 'things we have learned'.

What's wrong with just 'lessons'?

Well, you see, the problem with 'lessons' is it suggests being taught something by someone who imagines themselves as having superior knowledge, which is kind of outmoded and a little reactionary, whereas going forward* we want to create a culture of group-empowerment where we all make a journey of discovery and learning together in an interactive-fucking-whiteboard kind of way.

It's pleasingly ironic that a word like 'learnings' should convey to anyone – i.e. anyone who was taught proper lessons at school – the exact opposite of what it's supposed to mean.

---

*See outpouring of bile about 'Going Forward' on p.39.

Action/Task

● ●

'Can you action that, Steve?'
'The M4 corridor is a key sales area for us and
I've tasked Dave with this one.'

We all know who uses this sort of language: the go-ahead, dynamic middle manager who needs to ensure that his every utterance echoes with urgency and forward motion.

'Can you action that, Steve?' is not just a request for Steve to do the thing his boss has asked him to; it has a jump-to-it, right-now, I-wanted-it-yesterday feel about it. 'Action' it – go! This is a tough business, kill or be killed, take a dozen good men with you, sufficient ordnance, negate the threat, absorb collateral damage. But it says all this in a simple, non-threatening non-verb verb so that the middle manager can come across as a dispassionate, purely professional individual who doesn't lose his temper, keeps calm and gets the best out of his workforce (or co-workers). There is nothing more irritating in a work environment than the person who, in a real shit-hitting-fan situation, tries to appear above it all. 'I'm keeping my cool – there's no need to get personal about this, you seem very defensive.' I'm constantly amazed at the value accorded to keeping one's feelings hidden or in check in the workplace. If your work is worthwhile and important, then go ahead and lose your temper – what's the problem? If your work is essentially trivial, you'd be a fool to get worked up about it. I like to think I never lose my temper at work unless, like a child, I'm tired and/or hungry; the rest of the time I'm fairly sanguine because my work is ultimately pointless. But if you think soft-drink-vending machines or Nissan dealerships in Uttoxeter are really important, then lose your temper and don't get Steve to just 'action' it, tell him to fucking get on to it now!

'Task' comes from a slightly different perspective. It's saying: 'Hey, I know what's required – I've been there and done that, buddy. I know that what I'm asking you to do is difficult because I'm 360 degrees across this one. I see all, hear all, know all, so when I task you with maximising tavern snack sales in East Cheshire, believe me, I know what tough nuts they are to crack on the industrial estates in Congleton. I know how some of those guys in Knutsford can cut up rough. In fact, here's a dossier on all the major players in the Northwest business community sphere of operations.'

'Task' has acquired an even more sinister undertone in the last few years as jungle-based celebrity-torture game shows and dog-eat-dog job-interview programmes have dominated TV schedules. In these examples, 'task' implies that the task-setter knows your weaknesses and is in fact waiting for you to throw a wobbler and cock everything up, either by failing to eat the required number of kangaroo testicles, or ordering the wrong quantity of pickled onions as Project Manager. So, when your boss next mentions he is going to 'task' you with something, call him a tosser under your breath, and tread carefully.

Leverage

••

This is another one of those ghastly words that straddles the noun/verb divide. The financial world has taken a morally neutral term, normally applied to levers and fulcrums which maximise the effect of force applied, and turned it to the Dark Side. 'Leverage' in financial terms is using small amounts of your own money – and a lot of someone else's – to make a big purchase, which you otherwise couldn't afford.

If you were to ask an engineer or a mathematician or scientist, he'd probably say 'financial leverage' isn't actually 'leverage' at all as it doesn't take into account the cost of borrowing the money, i.e. the interest charged. In fact, I did ask one, via the internet, and this is what he replied:

Borrowing nullifies any leveraged effect as in the end, at the end of the debt contract, much more money will have been spent than would have been necessary if you had had all the money at the time of purchase. The cumulative effect over time of making the 'force' required multiplies higher, almost a reverse leverage. Appearances can be deceiving.

The poor mathematician, bless him, didn't realise that sharp operators in finance *hardly ever* pay the interest. In fact, it's unlikely that they ever really borrow the money in the first place. It's not the grammatical skulduggery involved with the use of 'leverage' as a verb or a noun that we should be worried about, or even the precise definition of the word in financial terms. It's enough to say that 'leverage' is some kind of hedge-fund villainy that financial con artists use to fuck other people over. They get their hands on borrowed money, which they haven't really borrowed, to buy stuff they never really own, which they then sell to unsuspecting – or occasionally quite suspecting but still desperately greedy – investors (occasionally an entire country like Greece), and which they then use to, as I say, totally fuck them over. It's as if they have bought a lovely cake for fourpence and sold it on as a Petri dish of smallpox for 80 billion pounds.

And this is perhaps why the word has acquired another meaning – that of using a particular position to gain advantage, say if you were negotiating a divorce settlement and threatened to withhold access to the children unless the other party agreed to your terms. Again, my internet mathematician said:

This is not really leverage. It's more like coercion than any physical application of force.

Actually, it's more like blackmail. And it's beyond me why

anyone not involved in that world would want to bring the dogshit of financial dealings into their house on the sole of their shoe by using the word 'leverage' for any purpose.

Parent

● ●

We're all familiar with the word 'parenting' – it's a catch-all term, covering what used to be known as 'bringing up children', i.e. feeding, clothing, educating, nurturing and generally caring for them. It's a horrible, inelegant-sounding word (a bit like saying 'feeting' instead of walking) and reeks of an early 70s liberal utopia; some kind of hippy commune, where we'd all come to our senses and abandoned the traditional nuclear family, with a father and a mother bringing up their own children, and instead pooled all the kids into a massive crèche, overseen by a group of specially appointed parent-monitors, wearing clothes that looked like Alpen, who would encourage them to weave and make dream-catchers and teepees.

For thousands of years, different cultures throughout the world seemed to manage child-rearing pretty well, just by passing on stuff called 'wisdom' from one generation to the next. But with the arrival of 'parenting' came the textbook that told you how to do it. Childcare manuals had been around for decades, many of them ridiculously harsh and overprescriptive. They were published at the rate of about one every ten years, with the occasional big splash being made by the likes of Dr Spock. But in the last quarter of the 20th century the genre has exploded and now the 'parenting' section of Waterstone's is about the size of Rutland. Cowering next to it is usually the section on philosophy and politics and, just like some massively influential political ideology, 'parenting' has fragmented into a range of loopy and ferociously passionate fringe parties and splinter-groups that would make the International Socialist Workers' Anarchist Faction proud. Feed on demand! Feed to a timetable! Give your life to your child! It's your life, take it back! Listen to your kids! Don't let them boss you around! Only feed vegetable mush! Let them eat meat! Only give them wooden toys! Splinters can kill! Road accidents really help a child's development! Don't let your child write with a pen until he's fifteen, ink is poison!

With all this bewildering advice swirling around them, it's no wonder that mothers and fathers throughout the world had little time for linguistic policing and the word 'parenting' was allowed to make itself useful doing odd jobs here and there and eventually get its feet firmly under the table. But we should never have allowed the horrible little gerund into the house because it has invited along for Christmas its even nastier cousin, the verb 'parent'.

I have found it quite difficult to give examples of the use of the verb 'parent'. It's like me trying to show you why I hate rollerblading; I can't quite pull off the mincing hip-swivel coupled with the punchable smug expression and, if I ever managed it, I would suddenly feel a deep sense of shame. Fortunately, help is at hand in the title of a childcare manual: *How to Parent* by Fitzhugh Dodson.

Fitzhugh's book may be terrific; in fact, I'm sure that anyone who doesn't balk at the verb in the title will be happy with a chapter called '*Playing with other children* – solitary, parallel, associate, cooperative'. And they surely won't blanch at a sentence like 'adolescence is a stage of tranquillity and disequilibrium'.

Interestingly, despite my assertion that the agenda of 'parenting' is to do away with the distinctions between mothers and fathers, Fitzhugh also wrote a book called *How to Father*. I suspect it's how to be a good father, not how to father a child, although I may be wrong and haven't yet caught up with that linguistic development.

Like any group of people who feel oppressed, some parents have become a tad militant in the last few years; finding a voice and claiming a lack of representation. Unfortunately, we all know about mumsnet and whatever the other one is called – menstum? – and their searing political interviews with Brown and Cameron about what type of biscuits and underpants they prefer, but there are many, many other groupings out there that cannot hide their sense of grievance. This is what Eve Sullivan, the Founder of *Parents Forum*, wrote on her website:

What I did not know, or realized only dimly then, was something that has become clearer and clearer to me over the years: parent is a verb.

'Parent is a verb' is defiantly declaimed from the mastheads of parents' blogs across America and increasingly Britain. There are so many things a parent has to do; it's active and physically draining *blah blah blah*. So it deserves to be a verb – a *doing* word.

At the bottom of this is a sense of injustice felt by parents that somehow their hard work is going unrecognised. Well of course it's unrecognised by children, but who else cares? All parents can hope for is that the rest of the world will make allowances for their faded looks, sagging bodies and limited range of conversation, but they cannot expect anyone to tolerate the butchery of the English language by the use of the verb 'to parent'.

Many modern words get more unacceptable the older you get...

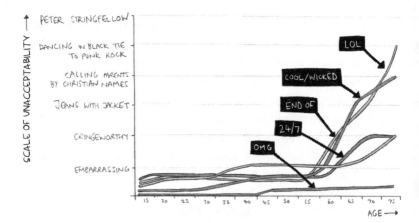

Going Forward

Some people now use this phrase quite unthinkingly, and so frequently it's become like a nervous tick or a clearing of the throat. And just like anyone with a Bluetooth headset, they've no idea what a tit it makes of them.

For others, though, 'Going forward' serves a definite purpose. Say there's a meeting. Let's imagine it's a disaster; everything is wrong, sales disappointing, profits low, no one will take our calls, everyone thinks we're crap. Then someone says, 'Going forward, how can we improve?'

'Going forward' comes from the world of positive thinking, optimism and can-do. 'Come on, guys, we can fix this!' But what's wrong with a bit of pessimism and despondency? Properly expressed, negative thoughts can be really liberating. 'We're shit and we know we are. Let's blame someone else, preferably someone not in the room that everyone dislikes – we'll all feel better after that.'

Going forward is like waving a magic wand. It's a Blairism – 'look, let's move on, draw a line under it'. You could see 'let's move on' etched in the lines on Blair's face as he struggled to promote his memoirs without mentioning Iraq, Blunkett, Mandelson, Campbell, Bernie Ecclestone, tuition fees, 24-hour licensing and … the Dome.

Why should we go forward? Why should we move on? Maybe we should dwell on the whole embarrassing experience (whatever it maybe) until everyone feels a little bit uncomfortable and starts squirming in their chairs. Then we might find out who screwed up and actually get somewhere. 'Moving on' and 'going forward' are all about the avoidance of conflict and confrontation on the terms of those who have least to gain from it. My father was a colliery manager in the 1970s and he loved confrontation; he thrived on it. OK, there were a lot of strikes at his pit, even over the mushy peas not being mushy enough, but everybody knew where they stood – squarely on opposite sides. After my father died, my uncle said confrontation was like a drug to him. There's not enough of that in management these days – if someone messes up something important, they should get shouted at; a proper bollocking. Whatever happened to those?

A huge part of our relationship with other people is devoted to avoiding offence; despite the success of post-war generations in dismantling old hierarchies and doing away with rules and taboos, nowadays it's easier than ever to do the wrong thing. In the modern workplace, just about the worst thing you can do is 'take it personally'. This is also known as being 'unprofessional'. But if you're pissed off about something, why not take it personally? Why not get angry? Perhaps the reddest rag to my bull is 'No need to be so defensive', which is nearly always followed by something like 'Going forward, how are we going to deliver more positive outcomes?' at which point, the most positive outcome would be a fist in the face.

Forever Home

●●●●●●●●●●●●●●●●●●●●●●●●●●●●●●●●●●●●●●●

This is one of Kirsty 'n' Phil's favourite sayings on *Location, Location, Location*, although Phil Spencer, poor chap, has a lot of twouble saying it. But I cannot be the only person who is instantly reminded by the rhythm of this horrid little phrase of Paul McCartney's contribution to one of the great musical crimes of the 20th century – 'The Girl Is Mine'.

At the end of this abysmal duet with Michael Jackson – which let's not forget appears on that great album *Thriller* (see Overrated Albums in *Can't Be Arsed*, still excellent value at £9.99) – Jacko and Macca do some tit-for-tat banter about who the 'doggone' (whatever that means) girl actually likes best. 'I'm a lover not a fighter' pleads the whey-faced gimp, but Paul's rejoinder is 'She told me I'm her forever lover'. I'm sure the word 'forever' had never been used in that way before and it shows, whatever you think about the morality of it, that Paul McCartney was a lyrical as well as a musical genius. It has a hideous, simultaneously buttock-clenching and emetic force, which loses virtually nothing in the passage of 30 years or so, until it pops up again in the mouths of two property expert toffs on a bewilderingly popular Channel 4 show about moving house.

But wait! What's this? My Wikipedia tells me that 'forever

home' is a term used in pet ownership in America. When you get a puppy from a breeder you are obliged to sign a form pledging you will be responsible for housing the mutt for the rest of its life. So it's no surprise that the gooey soppy language used by animal lovers has come to be shared by the kind of people who burst into tears over an en-suite bathroom, or when Kirsty and Phil get a couple of grand off the asking price for them.

However, as all soppy gooey pet owners know, you'll be lucky if your dog lasts you fifteen years. So the idea that anyone who is interested enough in property to watch an actual TV show about it would hang on to their house for that long, when they know they can make a massive profit by flogging their dream home after just a couple of years, is laughable.

Skill Set

My dictionary defines 'skill set' as 'a set of skills required to perform a particular task'. Fair enough, but what sort of context would it be used in?

'Jamie doesn't have the necessary skill set for this job.'

So, what function is the word 'skill set' performing in this context that 'skills' couldn't? You could say that 'skill set' is actually overqualified to perform the particular task of making it clear what someone is talking about when they use the phrase 'skill set'. Well, you could if you were an arse.

So the 'set' in 'skill set' is superfluous and redundant – so what? Isn't it better than giving you too little information? No – because it's an ugly phrase that has ugly connotations. 'Skill set' suggests that someone rather dislikeable, a management consultant almost certainly, has looked at a particular job and decided in their overpaid pseudo-scientific way exactly what is required to carry out a task, no more no less. We don't want to waste any money hiring someone overqualified, do we? So, a particular job is boiled down to a set number of tasks that are in turn boiled down to a set number of basic functions that need to be performed in a certain order. If we ascertain the various abilities of an individual within the company or a job applicant, we can tick off all the relevant skills this person has and allocate the job to the person who ticks the correct number of boxes.

There are hundreds of 'how to best present yourself' books and websites that claim to have some mystical and secret knowledge about the job market and devote whole chapters to 'understanding your skill set'. One declares: 'Making your "skill sets" clear to a prospective employer is a vital part of a successful job application.'

No – really? My job application is more likely to be successful if I tell the prospective employer what I can do? That's brilliant. I was planning on making him a collage or asking him to play backgammon.

Apparently what this means is that you are meant to quite methodically and objectively categorise your particular strengths. If you want to see someone in the very act of categorising their strengths, watch *The Apprentice* when one of the candidates is about to get fired: they start desperately listing their qualities, which turn out to be totally nebulous – 'I'm an excellent man-manager, I'm very good at strategy, I'm creatively strong, I meet deadlines, I thrive under pressure. I'm a winner.' The last one is always the killer.

Worshippers of the 'skill set' will claim that the *Apprentice* candidates are not listing their qualities properly at all. The 'skill set' should be a collection of objectively assessable qualities and strengths. A friend of mine in IT received a CV recently. Here is an extract from it:

Led the pitch process for all complex bespoke solutions both from a business & technical perspective working holistically with sales, account management, development & creative teams at all times. Rebranded XX's global online presence with extensive integrated e-marketing & reporting technology with complex business intelligence & multivariate marketing.

Apparently that means something in IT. 'And what's wrong with it?' cry the Skill Setters. 'Surely it's useful information?' Yes, if you want to recruit an automaton.

I sat on several BBC interview panels, all of which were attended by a member of BBC personnel, or BBC People, or whatever they're called now. Their job was to make sure no unfair questions were asked in the process – any questions which couldn't have been asked of all the other candidates. So I was totally out of order when I asked one bloke, who revealed he'd once been shot out of a cannon, what it felt like. Apparently, it wasn't a question I could have asked any of the other candidates. Of course, I *could* have asked them; it's just that their answers wouldn't have been as good. My wife has been on several interview panels for new teachers, at which a candidate's answers are monitored for the use of certain keywords. Drop in enough 'motivations', 'goal-centreds' and 'learning drivers' and the Deputy-headship of Humanities is yours.

All of these selection processes have the same aim as analysis by 'skill set'; to reduce the process to factual observable objective non-discriminatory tick boxes and to remove any decision based on whether you like the person, whether they have a tattoo, whether they seem pleasant, funny, clever in the right way and likely to get on with everyone else. If I ever get to interview anyone again, I have promised myself I shall at least be weeding out anyone using the term 'skill set'.

16

Step up to the Plate

● ●

This is a term from baseball – you know, the game where the World Series is contested by teams from only one country. In baseball, the 'plate' is the spot over which the pitcher must pitch the ball, and up to which the batter must step, if he is to have any hope of hitting it.

We have no claim to it whatsoever in the UK so no self-respecting Briton should be caught saying it, any more than they should say, 'We're going the whole nine yards here'; that rather embarrassing 80s dalliance with American football is thankfully over (sadly, I still remember the Superbowl parties). Baseball didn't even get its own Channel 4 series, so how 'step up to the plate' even crept into the language is a mystery.

The phrase, however, is creeping into serious news broadcasts as almost every on-air journalist seems to delight in demonstrating how hip they are with their grasp of the latest 'jive talk'. But 'step up to the plate' has its most ridiculous macho connotations in the workplace, where constant allusions to sport betray a total inability to express oneself properly, and the most mundane, meaningless meetings and administrative tasks assume epic proportions, e.g:

'We need the spreadsheet for this week's status meeting, Steve.
It's time to step up to the plate and get it sorted.'

or

'I need a thousand shelf-wobblers in Runcorn by Friday week – it's time
for the stationery guys to step up to the plate.'

It's a phrase much beloved by Keiths and Kens in industrial business parks all over the East Midlands and comes from the same lexicon as 'stick your head above the parapet' and 'I'm putting my cock on the block here' – all phrases that the clueless arrogant tossers wanting to win *The Apprentice* say when they become the Project Manager, as if outselling their rivals on a wet-fish stall in front of Lord Sir Alan of Electrotat is analogous with having a rock-hard baseball hurled towards your groin at 100 miles an hour. The day when one of them actually has the courage to say, 'I think it's my turn to assume responsibility,' I'll eat my own knuckles.

An interesting and appropriate footnote to the use and abuse of this phrase is the doomed attempt by the BBC to make a hideous daytime cookery game show called *Step up to the Plate* hosted by Loyd Grossman and Anton Du Beke. See? It's about cooking under pressure, what could be better? If you want to know what happened to that show, here's a Q&A lifted from the online listings magazine Digiguide.com:

Q. When's *Step up to the Plate* coming up on UK TV?
A. Unfortunately, *Step up to the Plate* isn't on the air any time soon.

'Any time soon' ... I think placing two such appalling expressions as 'step up to the plate and 'any time soon' so close together could actually cause a rip in the fabric of space-time.

Second-Phase Ball

• •

According to those who claim to be able to see a pattern in the game of rugby, there are several distinct phases of play: a psychotic eighteen-stone gorilla chucking the ball at a line of other lunkheads is the first phase and the second phase is when one of the lunkheads is tackled and there's 'breakdown'.

In short: the ball has been dropped and somebody else has picked it up. In the shambolic, mindless, eye-gouging, ear-ripping, scrotum-grabbing, hairy-arsed, homoerotic, simulated gangbang called rugby – the rules of which even its top-flight professionals don't understand properly – such random and chaotic events are dignified by technical-sounding terms like 'second-phase ball'.

'Scrum', 'ruck' and 'maul' are the operative words in rugby, all of which could be replaced by the more appropriate schoolboy term 'bundle'.

It's a complete mystery to me why anyone connected with a

sport, which they believe is tremendously exciting, would want to turn it into something dull like mechanical engineering or computer programming by using terms like 'second-phase ball'.

Professional sport is now awash with nutritionists, psychologists and sports scientists; people who used to be 'well built' are now deemed to have great 'upper-body strength', athletes fret over 'abdominal cores' and 'carb intake'. And on every football touchline, even at Saturday morning kids' level, someone is clutching a Lucozade Sport. When I was forced to play the game at school, all I had was this tasteless, clear liquid called water.

Just before the 1990 World Cup everyone was wondering what the hell John Barnes was on about when he advertised Lucozade Sport with the robotic phrase: 'It's isotonic, which means it's in tune with your body fluids.' Now Lucozade Sport has its own extensive website and team of sports scientists and nutritionists who will even come into your local school, if you like such things, and replace all the fun, excitement and unpredictability in your kids' kick-abouts with performance charts and bar graphs. The clue is in the name: Sports Science. It makes sport boring. And rugby doesn't need any help with that.

Can I Get?

● ●

I shudder every time I hear this appalling phrase. Whenever someone next to me in the queue at the coffee shop says, 'Can I get a decaf latte?' I'm willing the person behind the counter to reply, 'Where do you think you are, Greenwich Village? In Central Perk, waiting for Phoebe and Chandler to "rock up"? No, you can't get a decaf latte. It's my shop – I get the latte. You stand there and ask if you can HAVE a latte and I will get it for you and charge you £3.25. And that's for a take-away, not a take-out.'

Sadly, they never do. I would happily pay to have leaflets printed up and hand them out to the poor sods behind the counters who have to listen to this twat-speak a thousand times every day, but I don't because a) most of them are foreign and can't see what's wrong with it, and b) even English people don't care.

'It's such a small thing, it's only three words, why do you get so worked up about it?' say the Wishy-Washy. Well, it's like Parkinson's or MS – the little twitches and twinges on the extremities are signs that something bigger and more debilitating is coming.

If we don't stamp out transatlantic tosh like 'can I get' and 'take-out' pretty soon, we'll find our language has been seriously undermined by people saying 'Monday thru Friday', 'Happy Holidays' and 'Let's visit with each other'.

Some people think that Jay-Z, the popular rapping artist from Brooklyn, is responsible for increased 'can I get' usage, with his 1998 single 'Can I Get A ...' But you will find a strong argument on many of the internet chat rooms – in particular the ones I visit – based on individual words and phrases like 'can I get' (believe me they do exist), that Marvin Gaye's 'Can I Get a Witness' is a much older example of the trope.

Of the two I blame Jay-Z, as Marvin's need for a witness clearly indicates a conventional use of the verb 'to get' or 'fetch'.

Marvin is after a witness to what he thinks is criminal behaviour, 'cos his baby's treatin' him so bad. He wants the witness so badly he would be prepared to go and get one himself. Whereas Jay-Z asks: 'Can I get a FUCK YOU to these bitches from all of my niggaz?'

Clearly Mr Z assumes the FUCK YOU to the bitches to be forthcoming and does not expect to have to go and get one himself, as that would be demeaning to someone of his stature and it could even be interpreted as dissing on the part of the niggaz.

This is the horrible essence of 'can I get ...' It suggests you might be prepared to do something yourself whereas in reality you're expecting someone else to get their hands dirty for you.

So, if you are seated at a table in a restaurant and a waitress asks you what you would like, don't say 'Can I get the crispy pancakes and curly fries?' or whatever it is they are serving. Just say 'I would like ...' or even 'Please may I have ...' You are there to be served, after all, no need to get all rude about it. And when you walk into a pub, don't go up to the bar and say, 'Can I get a pint of Trussock's Old Dirigible?' say 'Can I have …' or, better still: 'A pint of your best foaming ale, please, landlord.'

How Good Is He?

● ●

I'm almost certain this was first coined by BBC's *Match of the Day* pundit Mark Lawrenson – he of the droll remark, hangdog expression and seemingly endless capacity to be bored by football matches he hasn't paid to watch.

'Lawro' used to have a double-act with John 'Motty' Motson in the commentary box for big live matches, during which Motty would babble away excitedly and Lawro would burst his balloon with a deadpan but slightly inappropriate one-liner, usually involving a lyric from an old pop hit. So Motty might cry, 'Belgium are launching attack after attack down the right-hand side and England seem powerless to stop it!' and Lawro would throw out something like: 'Talk about "Stop in the Name of Love".'

Motty would then giggle for a bit, then a Belgian would

dribble past a few England defenders and Lawro would say, 'Tell you what: how good is he?'

You have to hand it to the ex-pro football pundits, they have a genius for language. Alan Shearer has broken new territory with his vivid mixture of tenses in such gems as 'They should've went in two a-piece' and 'If he'd went to the keeper's left he scores'. Alan Hansen has elevated alliteration to new heights with 'pace, power, touch and technique, chance after chance, time and time again'. Tired of being ridiculed over the decades by smart-alec comedians for phrases they used as players like 'over the moon', 'sick as a parrot' and 'at the end of the day', they feel compelled to generate their own catchphrases.

But after years in the job, the studio pundits, as they often admit themselves, are 'running out of superlatives' even when they have all afternoon in a *Match of the Day* studio to think them up. So it's easy to imagine how the co-commentator, with 90 minutes of live football to gibber over, will turn to ever more ridiculous phrases like 'Tell you what …' followed by no information at all, and 'How good is he?'

Whenever I hear this phrase, I'm always tempted to shout back at the television, 'How rhetorical is that?'

Clearly 'How good is he?' requires no answer but its futile existence was born out of having two people sitting next to each other in a commentary box and neither of them having anything of any note to say to each other. What else is there to do but ask redundant questions?

The idea that a live football match needs even one person to speak incessantly for 90 minutes is infuriating enough. In the past, legendary pundits like David Coleman and Kenneth

Wolstenholme could go for at least 30 seconds without saying anything other than 'Oh, it's a goal!' or 'One-nil!' But nowadays someone like Simon Brotherton will prattle on and on for an entire game without drawing breath. And if that's not enough chatter for you, Mark Bright, Mark Lawrenson or Pat Nevin will tell you exactly what Simon Brotherton *has just told you* over slow-motion replays from five different angles.

To be fair to them all, the co-commentators are only obeying orders – the producers of live sport have clearly decided that the punters at home *love* the idea of an expert filling in the gaps in the commentator's knowledge, so throughout the game they are prodding the expert through the headphones to add 'colour commentary', even though the best most of them can manage is a dull grey. (ITV's 'Big' Ron Atkinson knew how to do the job properly, but his own particular brand of colour commentary was his undoing in the end.)

Probably the most enjoyable game at the dismal 2010 South Africa World Cup was the semi-final between Holland and Uruguay, because ITV's 'first choice' prattler, Jim Beglin, missed the match through illness. Clive Tyldesley was left on his own for the whole game and the brief passages of silence were golden. Except for the vuvuzelas.

There seemed to be light at the end of the football fan's tunnel when Lawro's knockabout comedy partnership with Motty was dissolved recently, but no. Guy Mowbray, Jonathan Pearce, Steve Wilson ... they've all had a crack at partnering Lawro to see who can revive the 'magic'. My feeling is Lawro should be given his comedy head and partnered with the people who will really appreciate his sense of humour – his long-lost cousins Paul and Barry Chuckle.

I'm Good

● ●

We're back to the *Friends* coffee bar:

> *'Hi, how's it going?'*
> *'I'm good.'*

Although, of course, if we were really in the *Friends* coffee bar, they'd be greeting each other with 'Hey!' (To which the grammatically correct response is 'What?')

For all I know, millions of people in Britain are already saying 'Hey' to each other – I clearly don't have my finger on the pulse if I'm still making *Friends* references.

I don't object to 'I'm good' on grammatical grounds: some people argue that the question 'How are you?' is a shortened form of 'How are you faring?' to which the answer must be an adverb like 'well' or 'poorly'. This misses the point entirely. Clearly, 'I'm good' is just a twattish thing to say.

Who is ever 'good' when someone asks them how they are? I think at best I'm fairly neutral. I would never rate myself as good at anything. It's just not for me to say and it demands the response 'I'll be the judge of that'. It reminds me of those TV chefs who, when they've turned out their lobster ravioli with basil sauce, have a taste and say, 'That is fantastic! Mmm ... those flavours! So delicious!' It reminds me of what my old schoolfriend Nigel would say: 'I love me, who do you love?'

I'd like to know what's wrong with 'I'm fine' as a reply. A lot of people seem to have trouble with 'fine' and 'nice' these days; they are apparently not nearly effusive enough in the age of 'awesome' and 'legend'. In fact, you can't get much better than 'fine' in its original sense of 'finished' or 'perfected'. For me, 'fine' is very close to 'quite good', which most people take as an offhand way of saying something is not that good at all or even a bit rubbish, but is actually almost the highest accolade I can give anyone or anything.

When it comes to greeting people, I'd like to know what is wrong with 'Alright'? It's multifunctional in that it can be phrased or interpreted as a question. If I say 'Alright?' to you, you might think I'm enquiring after your health, or telling you 'I'm all right'. You can even say 'Alright?' back as a question, simultaneously not answering my question and pretending to ask one yourself. Two people nodding and saying 'all right' to each other as they pass in the street tells both parties all they need to know: the other person has acknowledged their presence and is unlikely to want them to stop and chat; they are not suffering from a serious illness, nor are they ridiculously happy and pleased with themselves to the point where you are expected to ask them why. Let's start a campaign – All You Need Is Alright.

21

Rock Up

When someone says they are going to 'rock up' it usually means they are going to turn up, or simply arrive, at a function casually or without any prior arrangement or invite. 'Is there a dress code or can I just rock up?' or 'If the party starts at 8 p.m., I'll probably rock up before ten. Because, you see, I don't really care much for your uptight conventions of smart clothes and punctuality and I said "rock" as in rock music – cool and unconventional, and maybe a little bit naughty.'

These naughty people may not be aware that to 'rock up' is also, in certain circles, 'to smoke or manufacture crack cocaine'. No doubt that would make the phrase even more appealing to them because drug users and dealers are, like, well you know, cool? Of course, the people who like to say 'rock up' are free and easy-going characters; young, unfettered and 'mad for it', that's how they talk, so what's the problem? None, I suppose, as long as they don't come anywhere near me or my family. Which, to be fair, is unlikely. What I really do object to is the spread, and usage, of the phrase 'rock up' by people I am likely to encounter, i.e. colleagues at work and people who wouldn't be found dead in a crack den or a mosh pit.

I work in a fairly dull office, where there are people who

frequent a techie/geek website called The Register, which recently carried an article with this heading:

Will a service pack for Windows 7 rock up any time soon?

When I saw this sentence I nearly vomited, but not before I took my hat off to the sub-editor of the website for managing to cram two of my most hated expressions into five words (see 'Any Time Soon', p. 91). It shows you just how deep the crisis in the English language has become when a geeks' forum for technology, software and other such baffling nonsense can embarrass itself in this way.

The problem with The Register is that it is originally a British website, which has become infested by the supposedly cooler nerds with skateboards from California. It also likes to think of itself as an anti-establishment and subversive site, hence its slogan 'Biting the hand that feeds IT'. Yeah, you tell 'em, guys! Now hear this, World Wide Web, The Register is really sticking it to Windows 7 and fighting back against The Microsoft Man!' You can imagine the kind of fizzing wise-crackery that goes on in their offices: 'I might just rock up to the stationery cupboard and score some toner for the HP 1300.' 'Hey, the new JavaScript patch really smashed it.' 'Dude, I just totally maxed out my USB dongle.'

You might think that IT boffins are the last people on earth who should be bandying around phrases like 'rock up', but how about a choirmistress from Harrogate in Yorkshire? A lady called Rhiannon Gayle has set up a choir called 'Rock Up and Sing' to which you can just 'rock up' and start singing. On the face of it, it's a very clever name: the rehearsals for the choir are informal and free from snobbery – you can indeed just 'rock up', and the songs they sing are indeed rock songs, or what the *X Factor*'s interpretation of a rock song would be – Journey, Billy Ray Cyrus and *Joshua Tree*-era U2.

But however clever or appropriate the name, Rhiannon is forgetting one thing – she lives in Yorkshire. People in Yorkshire do not say 'rock up'. It's against their very nature. They don't like to turn up to things casually, at any time they feel like and without the proper footwear or overcoat. And to try to encourage them to 'rock up' is like trying to tempt Eve to eat the apple – it's the beginning of a great fall down a deep depressing shaft into a bottomless pit of despair and hopelessness. So shame on you, Rhiannon. Having said all that, it's just what you'd expect from Harrogate. If people in Leeds or Barnsley had been found 'rocking up' to anything, I would have been prepared to throw in the towel and admit my powerlessness to halt the spread of such bullshit. Harrogate may well be in Yorkshire but, oh, how it wishes it was in Surrey. The lack of any heavy industry or discernable accent and the predominance of four-wheel drives and gastropubs betray a yearning for the soft southern lifestyle and its easy ways with dress codes and punctuality. It may well be best for all concerned if Harrogate could be somehow deported from the rest of the county, so that the remaining Tykes can be preserved from these sinister changes to the language. He could then serve the nation as a kind of coal-mine canary which if it fell off its perch underground was a sure indicator of the spread of poisonous gas. So, if the people of Yorkshire (minus Harrogate) are ever found to be using phrases like 'rock up', that's the signal that the rest of the country will know it's time to surrender.

Swing By

This originated as a term from space exploration, meaning the use of the gravitational pull of a planetary body to change a satellite or spacecraft's direction. So, if NASA wanted to send a probe to Neptune, they'd probably take a 'swing-by' off Uranus.

Over the course of a few years, this has mutated into:

> *'We could meet up later.'*
> *'Where will you be?'*
> *'I'll be in Starbucks.'*
> *'OK, I'll swing by in ten. Can I get a flat white?'*

We are forced to imagine that the life of someone who might 'swing by later' is so full of possibilities for scintillating conversation, cocktails, fine food, wine, sex and international travel that they might just be too busy to grace us with their presence.

Like a lot of these phrases, the hatefulness of the user is possibly all in my head. Don't most people use 'swing by' in all innocence as an alternative to 'popping round'? Well, let's try putting 'swing by' into some more innocent 'popping round' contexts and see how absurd that claim is:

> *'I'm just going to swing by the newsagents for the* Daily Express *and some tampons.*

> *'I noticed you've not been out much recently, Mrs Ferguson, so I thought I'd swing by and see how you are.'*

> *'I was so sorry to hear about your husband – I felt I had to swing by and offer my condolences.'*

There is no way you could just casually use 'swing by' in any of these contexts. You would have to really give it some thought, like premeditated murder; unless, of course, you are so used to saying it that it has become second nature and you have become in effect an habitual criminal, in which case you are the wrong sort of person for me to be seen with so I'm going to stop talking to you now.

Fashion Forward

This is supposed to mean someone or something that is ever so slightly more 'with it' than anyone or anything that is fashionable right now. 'Fashion forward' is not merely fashionable, it's fashionable before dullards like us have even thought of it.

'Fashion forward' is not ridiculous, you see, it's cooler than cool. Obviously not everyone who is described as 'fashion forward' turns out to be cool. They are the ones who embrace trends which never catch on – like corset jeans (really), or two ties and shirts at once (yes, really) or pop star Rhianna's diamante eye patch (Gabrielle road-tested that one, already) or Beyoncé with her fringed spectacles.

She thinks that arse of hers can excuse any number of ludicrous actions but it can't, love, I'm sorry.

So you can't be too 'fashion forward' because everyone might think you're a clown, like Vivienne Westwood, or whoever designed Home Secretary Theresa May's signature spaceman coat.

Although try telling that to people who 'know' about fashion. The judgement on whether someone is fashionable or clownlike is not made by people like you and me – it's made by the fashion fops themselves. So, as long as the people who are 'in' say something's 'fashion forward', it is.

But all they are creating is a hierarchy of fools. His guitar is loud but mine is one louder – mine goes up to eleven. Her hat is tall and pointy but mine is taller and pointier.

Ambitious people in fashion are like ambitious people everywhere else. While constantly struggling and striving to be better than their contemporaries, they are also straining and stretching language to describe exactly *how much* better they are than their contemporaries. So you get characters (read: clowns) on *The Apprentice*, who are trying to save their own skin at the expense of someone else, claiming, 'I'm not a one-trick pony; I'm not even a ten-trick pony. I'm a field of ponies.'

People who make statements like this can't resist passing on the benefit of their wisdom. Here's an example from a business guru's blog:

If you're able to get ahead of the game in your industry or your niche, you're able to know what's coming next. If you know what's coming next and people see that, it will be only a matter of time before you start to rise up in your community as the leader and authority on the subject.

So being ahead of the game is what it's all about. Pick the winner before anybody else has spotted its potential; spot a trend before the next chump. Start wearing flip-flops with a tuxedo or spectacles with a lampshade fringe before the crowd catch on and 'you'll rise up in the community as a leader and authority on the subject'. But most of the time being ahead of the game is a gamble. You might think you're miles ahead of your competitor on the running track, only to find you're actually a whole lap behind him and everyone's laughing at you.

Über

The hyperbole and excess of the fashion industry has pushed the use of superlatives literally beyond what the language can bear. 'Über', meaning 'over' or 'above', is now the basic unit of measurement for the fashionasties. There are über-stylists, über-models, über-fashion critics and the actor Robert Pattinson, apparently, has 'one of the top ten über-unkempt hairdos'.

The allure of 'über' for the twatterati (my own ridiculous word that combines glitterati with twat) lies in those two dots over the 'u'. The umlaut smacks of the Germanic or the Nordic or the Scandinavian – anywhere where the women are tall, blonde and powerful with impeccable cheekbones and the photographers and designers are stern and precise. All very tempting for fashionable freaky people and it helps explain why

David Bowie was so keen to ponce around Berlin in the mid-70s.

But now 'über' has spilled over into the vocabulary of normal people, who are using it as an everyday substitute to describe extreme examples of anything at all and bugger the umlaut. Mothers outside my kids' school playground say they won't allow their own children to walk home from school because they are 'über-cautious'. I'm tempted to reply that I'm neither cautious nor reckless; in fact I'm über-indifferent.

The shallowness of the über-user today can best be seen in the pages of the website which is named after the word itself. Über is, inevitably, an online Celebrity Beauty Shop. It sells face cream, tanning spray, eye gel, foaming bath milk and high-gloss anti-frizz serum, all endorsed by Peaches Geldof, Ashley Simpson, June Sarpong and Davina McCall, who says: 'I look after my skin with Über Sassy Celebrity Face Cream.' I had to keep clicking through the pages in the desperate hope that somebody like Charlie Brooker or The Onion magazine had set the whole thing up as a piss-take, but no – sadly it's real and clearly shifting quite a lot of face-spritz and knee-balm. To be fair to the makers of Sassy Celebrity Face Cream, they have maintained the umlaut on Über – and turned it into a pair of eyes giving a cheeky wink over a smiley-face 'U'. What more could you want from your celebrity face cream?

On Trend

· ·

To show just how difficult it is to keep up with changing fashions, the fashion industry keeps updating the word for fashionable. So what used to be 'with it', 'trendy', 'fab', 'groovy', 'happening' or 'gear' is now 'on trend'. Defenders of the rubbish people speak nowadays will argue that all words are subject to fashion and the fact that all the words I listed just now are out of date proves the point that language is constantly evolving, not just in the world of fashion but everywhere, and I am just grumbling about words and phrases that belong to a new generation, not my own, and indeed just becoming plain crotchety about getting old.

Of course, all that is true *but* it's the nature of the new words being coined that really gets up my pipe. Take 'on trend' – why use a dull and statistical word to describe something as flamboyant and energetic as fashion? It conjures up an image of x and y-axes and parabolic curves with a vertex and a median point and somewhere amid a blur of numbers is the point at which something is 'on trend'.

The intention behind 'on trend' is to make it clear to anyone with money to spend that they absolutely have to buy that particular item of leopard-print because the scientists in the fashion lab have conclusively proven that, right at *this* moment, leopard-print is 'on trend'.*

The phrase itself also sounds suspiciously like 'on message' – the language of Clinton and *The West Wing* enthusiastically adopted by Blair and Campbell and Mandelson – which denotes a party line that must be parroted at all costs under any circumstances. Everyone speaking on behalf of the government was obliged under pain of a massive bollocking, followed by political oblivion, to regurgitate whatever limited, single-sentence sound-bite had been endorsed at the time. So what does 'on trend' say other than you step off the agreed swatch card of colours and fabrics at your peril?

This is why all of a sudden all the mums at the school gates (I hang around there a lot) have, over the years, arrived en masse wearing sunglasses that make them look like owls, or 'the' gypsy skirt from Primark or skinny jeans or ankle boots or harem pants. The fear of not having the right stuff – of not being 'on trend' – reminds me of the cycling proficiency test that all kids had to take at school at around ten years old. Part of the test was to try to ride your bike along a flattened fire-hosepipe. I was so worried about falling off that I was never actually on it for more than two seconds. Following fashion can be the same disconcerting experience for many people, which is probably why, despite their willingness to make themselves look stupid in an attempt to keep up with fashion, most of them will avoid 'fashion forward' (see above) like the plague.

---

*Of course leopard-print will have gone by the time anyone reads this, but give it a couple of years and it will be back, like a cold sore.

But I think people should really stop worrying. You don't need to be 'on trend' or 'fashion forward' or ever even vaguely 'in touch'. My wardrobe is quite simple. I don't have many clothes but everything in my collection goes with everything else. Some people might call it a capsule wardrobe in the sense that I might as well have been blasted into space for 20 years and come down to earth again wearing exactly the same things. All my clothes are in a 'medium' and are either grey, black or blue; they have no patterns or logos and they all arrive in the post. Anything with surplus pockets or flaps or buttons gets sent back and anything I like I reorder twice. Or rather my wife does. This saves me a great deal of embarrassment and inconvenience; I heartily recommend it.

Judgement Call

I make a judgement, you make a judgement, Dickhead from *The Apprentice* makes a 'judgement call'. Or he displays cowardice and says, 'I can't make that judgement call' – for which he may later be punished by Lord Alan in the boardroom, at which point he can 'hold his hands up' and 'step up to the plate' and admit that he made a tough 'judgement call' to not make the 'judgement call'.

Just like, 'at this moment in time' or 'track record', 'judgement call' is an utterly pointless tautology ('pointless tautology' might also be one itself, I'm not sure).

But whereas the first two could possibly arise from laziness, I think people who say 'judgement call' really mean to say it, because they think it makes them look like they're 'on it'.

The kind of person who says 'judgement call' is the kind of person who is prepared to *make* a 'judgement call'. They're in at the sharp end, at the coal face, eyeball to eyeball, prepared to go *mano-a-mano* with the guy from sales and distribution and he wants to know whether the sales and distribution guy will want three vans with 30 boxes of staples to go to Kettering or two vans with 45 boxes and if the guy from sales and distribution can't make that 'judgement call' then dammit *he* will.

Whether the people in sales and distribution are prepared to go for a few drinks after work with this kind of guy or whether they think he's a complete moron to be avoided at all costs is a matter of judgement.

Team GB

Did you know this is now the official name of Great Britain's Olympic Team? Can you believe it? I'm telling you it's true – 'Team GB'. It may even be officially written as 'teamgb' in hideous lower case – the kind of naff graphics gimmick everyone was trying in the late 90s. It's about as cutting edge as using the @ symbol in a brand name or a title. Who can forget Hale and Pace's *H&P@bbc*? I wish I could.

Here's a great example of how the world of business is mangling our language and is yet another indictment of the tits at the top of British sport, who seem to think they have something to learn from it:

The Development Team within @UK PLC is dedicated to producing quality software solutions. Our quality management system is based on the

*ISO 15504 standard for software development process improvement.
We also use the DSDM methodology where appropriate, to ensure we
work to time and to budget.*

You may be wondering who @UK PLC are and what they do. So am I. It's impossible to tell. It's the kind of impenetrable and infuriating brand/product/company name that is spreading throughout British life. They could be anybody; @UK PLC might well be the new name for Tottenham Hotspur, such is the extent to which 'business' has infected sport.

'Team GB' came into being at the Beijing Olympics and no one in authority raised an eyebrow. Neither Adrian Chiles, Clare Balding nor even Huw Edwards lifted a finger or, in Huw's case, curled a lip to stop it. They could have just ignored it, just like everyone ignored Paul Ince when he insisted he be called The Governor. But no, they all chirped away merrily about the increasing medal haul of 'Team GB' in the totally useless sports of yachting, clay pigeon shooting and riding silly bikes, as the Great Britain of David Hemery, Brendan Foster, Daley Thompson and er … the big Northern Irish lass was consigned to the historical dustbin of Proper Names For Things. Does anyone remember 'university', usurped by the pathetic 'uni'? or how the Royal Mail was somehow allowed to briefly become Consignia, and Mr Dog, the best-named dog food ever, was swallowed by 'Cesar' (not even spelt correctly)?

As far as I'm aware one lone voice protested about 'Team GB': Sky Sports' *Soccer Saturday* presenter Jeff Stelling. In an impassioned rant at the top of the show one Saturday, to the total bemusement of pundits Paul Merson and Matt Le Tissier,

Jeff sounded off about the nonsense of calling a sports team 'Team' anything. 'We know it's a team! Please stop it!' he cried. As always, Jeff was bang on. The 'team' prefix on 'Team GB' is indeed supposed to suggest teamwork and it's staggeringly inappropriate for the Great Britain athletics team for two reasons.

First, the team tag is a common device used by businesses to encourage collective responsibility and behaviour in the workplace, hence you have 'daily scrums' and team bonding/building sessions. They appropriate the language of sport to make their ghastly existence sound more interesting than it is. So why would a sport need to appropriate the language of sport to make it sound more sporty? If they are so bewitched by the bollocks-speak of business, why don't they call themselves British Athletics Incorporated or Competitive Physical Solutions UK Ltd: 'We have a passion for excellence'?

Second, and despite all the above, proper teams play proper team games like football and cricket; athletics is an individual competition. The point of the Olympics is to celebrate *individual* achievement – nationalism was only nailed on in the late 19th century. Clearly, any sport that can be played by a team should be excluded from the Olympics, as well as all those stupid yachting and cycling events that 'Team GB' seem to be so good at. As I'm sure they would say, that would put a big hole in their bottom line.

28

Jedward (et al)

● ●

Crasis, elision, contraction – whatever you call this linguistic device, it's the work of the Devil. Well no, not the Devil exactly; rather the work of a much more subtle and insidious entity. It's not possible to pin the blame for jamming-together-two-perfectly-acceptable-words-to-make-another-hideous-one on a particular journalist or commentator. I'm sure there are many that claim the credit but I prefer to think that there is some kind of sinister, manipulative creature which has burrowed its way into Western civilisation; some offspring of a succubus and a basilisk mated with one of the 3am Girls that simultaneously implants and nurtures shitty ideas into the heads of people who write about, talk about and watch television, films and pop music, which are then regurgitated in the name of 'just a bit of fun'. The creature must have considerable hypnotic powers to enslave the millions of readers of *Heat* and *Grazia* and the viewers of ITV2, BBC3 and *So Graham Norton*, because everyone appears to want to participate in 'the fun'; even people's nans are calling Susan Boyle SuBo.

Social Commentators (whatever they are) will put the spread of this kind of language down to the power of The Brand. Jennifer Lopez has her own perfume, her own range of clothing, she's even probably patented the shape of her own arse, so isn't J-Lo a really neat way to say her name AND a marketable logo? It might be for the desperate hacks and shysters who depend on Jennifer Lopez's career but why does everyone else have to join in? Why do people fall for The Brand's trickery – even when they've been made fully aware of what it's playing at? It's as mystifying to me as the people who feel no shame in parading around in clothing, the very existence of which is to promote the logo of the company that made it?

From its humble origins as a burn-mark on a cow's backside, The Brand has grown into one of the most overused words and unpleasant concepts in the English language. You only have to type Brand into Google or Wikipedia and, as if you had typed in bestiality by mistake, you are instantly bombarded with the most appalling language and hideous flowcharts.

OMG! BENNIFER IS SO OVER!

The concept of The Brand is attached totally inappropriately and meaninglessly to people, places, television programmes, abstract concepts, even marriages. Brand Beckham, i.e. the married couple David and Victoria, is a phrase conjured up by the very people who want it to spread into common usage. In cahoots with the people who print a snapshot of them every time they put on another pair of oversized sunglasses, the Beckhams and their 'people' encourage talk of the pair of them as a Brand in order to shift more product.

It's probably the same for Brangelina and Bennifer. Boris Johnson has the unique ability to appear a half-wit while being five times cleverer than everyone else, so he is probably perfectly happy with BoJo. The oddly quiffed tit twins John and Edward (or Jedward) seem too stupid to be aware of anything that's going on around them but I doubt Susan Boyle ever had any inkling that people would a) want to turn her into a brand name or b) find the words 'Susan' and 'Boyle' too time-consuming to say without abbreviation.

The amount of time it takes to say a word seems to have more and more influence on the way we speak (see 'End Of' p. 219 and '24/7' p. 175). We seem to be obsessed with saving time – the door-close button in lifts was only invented to give people the illusion that they could speed up the lift-moving process; computer programs are designed so that the response to clicking on a link is measured in fractions of a second. The time saved is crucial; with all that saved time we can do … what exactly? Relax? No – we just fill that time with more stuff. With text and email it's easier to communicate faster. But the time saved by these rapid forms of communication is not used by people to make their communication more thoughtful and lengthy. It's encouraged even more truncated exchanges.

But if we have to be brief there's no need to be stupid as well. The great Roman historian Tacitus had a way of speaking clearly and plainly and beautifully; he gave his name to taciturn, the living embodiment of which is the Yorkshireman. He will be brief and eloquent without being embarrassing, leaving you in no doubt as to his meaning or intentions. Perhaps there could be some kind of smartphone app for text and email that converts the shoddy abbreviated nonsense we use into proper succinct English. I've got the perfect name for it – 'Appen.

Back in the Day

• •

It's astonishing how many young people use this phrase to refer to something that happened about 18 months ago. 'Oh yeah, Gordon Brown – he was prime minister back in the day.' It's a phrase which the Homeric Bard might have legitimately used at the beginning of the *Iliad* to describe a row between the gods at the dawn of time, but your emo-haired pan-arsed, pants-flashing 22-year-old idiot can't remember much further back than last week, so 'back in the day' has come to mean 'when people used number keys to text each other'.

But what also annoys me about 'back in the day' is the way the phrase itself evokes a completely different set of experiences from what British youth are used to.

'Back in the day' has a ring of *Huckleberry Finn* and *Stand By Me* about it. It's the school prom revisited by Marty McFly or the teenage years of George Bailey's *Wonderful Life*. It's just about acceptable to hear it from an American. But the British memory is full of tea cosies and balaclavas; death-trap fridges and lockjaw. Well, mine is, anyway, and there's nothing in the scrapbook of memories for today's youth to get too misty-eyed about either: nostalgia for a 22-year-old probably consists of Tony Blair, *Teletubbies*, Tamagotchis and the death of Diana.

But the young have now claimed the phrase for themselves. The sagacious broadcaster Clive Anderson once complained that a young person told him he was too old to use the phrase 'back in the day'. I quite agree: someone of Clive's intellect and gravitas should know better, but I'm also sympathetic to his complaint that he has more right to the phrase as he is old enough to appreciate how long ago 'the day' should be.

It is in the interests of young people that they correct the notion that they have memories of sticklebacks. I thought help was at hand when I stumbled across the internet-based 'back in the day' calculator. The creator was becoming increasingly annoyed by people using 'back in the day' to describe a wide range of time, almost to the point that 'back in the day' seems to be just a good day someone once had.

He goes on:

At happyrobotUSA, setting and obeying standards is important to us, so we have built an official and nationally sanctioned 'back in the day' calculator. Select the year you were born, press submit, and via computers on the 'internet' we will tell you your own individual time frame for 'back in the day'.

All well and good – I typed in my own birth year, 1961, to be told by the calculator that 'back in the day' for me was between 1994 and 1996. Apart from feeling slightly challenged as a 50-year-old to remember further back than 17 years, the very idea that my dimly remembered but surely golden past was when I was between the ages of 33 and 37! By then I was already comfortably dull. I'd formed the opinion that any holiday destination which took more than two hours travelling time couldn't possibly be worth the effort (read more in *Can't Be Arsed* – still excellent value at £9.99), that supermarket curries are better than restaurant curries, that it's too much trouble to go to the cinema to watch a film, that an empty room should never have a light on and that any purchase over £9 required serious thought. And by then I was already going 'urrrgghhh' when I sat down in an armchair.

Not that the teenage or the late-twenties me was any more exciting. To be honest, the best thing I can remember about myself as a younger person is that I was further away from old age and death than I am now.

Me Time

● ●

If you read enough women's magazines and Sunday supplement features you'll be aware of the concept of 'me time'. It's time devoted to oneself, but unlike similar new-age-therapy bollocks phrases such as 'take a swim in Lake You' it is not used as a jokey reference to a person's self-centred neediness. It's taken seriously, particularly by those journalists and PR people promoting self-indulgent products like health spas, high-fibre cereals, beauty parlours, bubble bath, chocolate, chocolate drinks, certain types of yoghurt and jewellery.

Apparently, only women are allowed 'me time' because, they argue, men have been enjoying it for the last 300,000 years (don't they deserve it? The wheel didn't invent itself, love). It's also important to understand that, strictly speaking, not *all* women are entitled to 'me time', just the ones who have children. You will find a lot of wittering about 'me time' on mumsnet. The childish, petulant foot-stamp implicit in the phrase tells you all about the frustration and bitterness of women who feel that having children, rather than bringing fulfilment to their life, has somehow cheated them out of it. 'Me time' is the sort of thing a tantrum-ing toddler shouts when his older brother has had two minutes on the swing: 'Me want it!

Me do it! Me time!' But the mothers and journalists who use the phrase argue that there's no shame in demanding a break from the children, claiming 'self-preservation is not self-indulgence'.

This break can involve either sitting around an expensive spa hotel in oversized, fluffy, white dressing gowns or locking yourself in the bathroom with some floating candles and a hot chocolate. Anything really which recaptures the feeling of being in an overflowing roll-top tub with a Cadbury's flake, auditioning the finger puppets.

Nobody wants the nation's mothers to return to the days when they either stuck the screaming baby in a pram at the bottom of the garden or their head in the gas oven to get a bit of peace. But what has happened is that the marketing people have, like a kestrel that detects a dormouse fumbling with a hazelnut from a mile high, spotted an opportunity to sell premium-priced crap to susceptible women. QVC could easily be renamed 'The Me Time Channel', devoted as it is to selling luxury indulgence products, snuggle blankets, essential oils, massage mitts, mineralising muds and scented candles.

Women don't have to behave like Joan Collins in *Dynasty*, swanning around in a turban demanding to be served drinks on a tray by a bare-chested Chippendale wearing only a bow tie. Of course they should have a break from the children occasionally. I'm happy to spend most of Saturday with my kids, watching them play *FIFA 11* for a couple of hours or *Final Score* on the red button, while my wife takes it easy for a bit. And there are acceptable ways to make it clear that's what she wants: 'I'm going for a lie down' or 'I'm going out, get your own bloody tea' followed by a door slam. But never 'I'm going away to have some "me time".'

Anything
Kathy Lette Says

Kathy Lette is the Australian author and journalist who has been variously described as an 'Australian National Treasure' and 'the most tedious Australian personality ever created'. To be honest I think the word 'Australian' is redundant there but, if you're not sure which side of the fence you're on, have a look at these quotes.

1. Women want to be treated as equals not sequels.
2. Men have black belts in tongue fu.
3. Women suffer from facial not racial prejudice.
4. For women wordplay is foreplay.
5. How come men are so good at finding the remote control but can't find the clitoris?

She's playing out the same basic man-hating shtick as the first alternative female stand-ups 30 years ago, but with a twist in that she seems to have a form of Tourette's syndrome, which means she can't stop quipping. The puns and the double entendres are endless – 'I'm named after a diary and I've had many entries' – and it's not just in print: if you've ever heard her interviewed on the radio or television she's always at it (fnaar fnaar). She even has a daily updated page on her website called 'Quiplash' (doesn't mean anything but sounds like it does) which usually carries 'Men are from Mars but women prefer a Finger of Fudge'-type aphorisms.

Kathy Lette is very popular, rich and successful and I don't (genuinely) have a problem with clever, funny women taking the piss out of men – if only there were more and better ones. Like Joan Rivers – a great comedian. She may have an equally predictable stance when it comes to men but she is properly funny; she does strong material and shocking one-liners and she's not constantly trying to reinvent the language by jamming two words together and forcing them to copulate. And that's my big beef with Kathy Lette, because she has influenced the style of a great many female columnists, who are all keen to impress with their own versions of Kathy's 'tongue fu', 'nom du porn' and 'celebritocracy'. Indeed, it's impossible to get through a day's papers without being assaulted by a least half a dozen new ones. Some upmarket broadsheets run regular competitions inviting submissions for a new crop of neologisms and encouraging their readers to spread twat-speak like 'glibido', 'osteopornosis' and 'inoculatte' – all of which translate as: you're trying too hard.

32

Frenemy

●●●

Another one of those words that is supposed to make you feel clever when you drop it into conversation. It shows you've been reading the *Sunday Times Style Supplement* or some hard-faced *Daily Mail* columnist or even Kathy Lette. Surprisingly, it was first coined as long ago as 1954 by the syndicated columnist Walter Winchell. Doubly surprising as Winchell was using it to refer to the Russians and these days it's almost exclusively used to describe a particular type of female.

To find out which type, take a look at some of the examples of frenemies given on Wikipedia: Miley Stewart and Amber & Ashley in *Hannah Montana* – these are rivals in an American tween soap and are basically bitchy teenage girls. Or there's Serena and Blair in *Gossip Girl* (an American soap/sitcom for slightly older teenagers), who are basically some bitchy teenage girls. Or there's Susan Meyer and Edie Britt in *Desperate Housewives* (an American soap/sitcom for adults), who are basically some bitchy women.

'Frenemy' evokes a horrible notion of sisterhood where all the upfront signs are cordial and supportive but underneath they want each other to fail desperately. So, in effect, it's a cowardly way of saying 'two-faced cow'. It also reveals a rather unhealthy desire to categorise people in a way that almost legitimises the behaviour. If someone is being nice to your face and all the while doing their best to undermine you and rejoice in your failure you're either working in television and there's not much to be done about it, or you could just dump the person and stop being friendly to them. By calling them a 'frenemy' you're not making a decision, a 'judgement call' (if you prefer), about whether they are a friend or not; you're actually making a bit of a joke out of it and admitting to yourself that you do quite like them, so you probably deserve each other.

Inappropriate

Behaviour or language which is deemed 'inappropriate' is supposed to be offensive or unacceptable – except in a lot of cases it's neither; it's just something that many people who use 'inappropriate' don't like; people like council officials, social workers, some teachers, politicians and BBC apparatchiks. They don't like it because it oversteps certain boundaries established by a bizarre politically correct orthodoxy with which they have been indoctrinated as if it were a new religion. It's an attempt to set some objective standard of behaviour without using the words 'right' or 'wrong' because to do so would suggest some kind of objective morality. But a lot of people who use the word 'inappropriate' don't really believe in objective morality, they believe in an agenda; an agenda which excludes having opinions, raising your voice, complimenting members of the opposite sex on their appearance or talking about God.

Other people, including some journalists and news organisations, use 'inappropriate' precisely because they want to *avoid* being judgemental. If you put 'inappropriate' into Google you get a massive amount of stuff you don't necessarily want to see. It appears to cover racist and sexist language as well as, inevitably, pornographic material. To call any of it 'inappropriate' seems to be slightly wet and weaselly. It's as if no one wants to own up and say something is smutty or ugly, vile or just plain grotesque.

Take the *X Factor* final of 2010, which in the nine-hour build-up to the non-event (concluding with the *even more* anticlimactic victory by painter and decorator Matt Cardle) featured live performances from two very famous trollops wearing very few clothes, simulating sex and showing off as much of their bodies as legally allowable by Ofcom. This all took place in front of a massive TV audience, about 50 per cent of which would have been girls under twelve. There was widespread public outrage, but the only way the media felt able to describe it was by calling it 'inappropriate'. The last thing the tabloids want to appear is prudish and in this context 'inappropriate' means 'Of course, we all liked it but it's not really for kids.'

In the same way, to call a racist joke 'inappropriate' is a bit like 'oohing' at an edgy comic in a comedy club. Usually people only 'oooh' to let the person sitting next to them know that they didn't think it was funny (but they did, really). Despite the fact that 80 per cent of the population are racist and a lot of racist jokes can be quite funny, a racist joke is still bad. To call it 'inappropriate' just doesn't do the job and as an adjective it's quite ... well, 'inappropriate'.

Issues

'Issues' are problems. If something is a problem, say it's a problem. A generation has grown up using the word 'issue' because they've been taught that saying something is a problem is somehow negative. An issue can be skirted around and talked out without hurting anyone's feelings or apportioning blame, but what's wrong with blame if blame is due? Steve has telephone manner 'issues'. So why not say to him: 'Steve, there is a problem with your telephone manner – people think you're a dickhead.'

Using 'issue' is OK if the sense is 'the issue of benefit scroungers' where there is a genuine debate about what we should do about and how we should describe people on benefits. Or we may be discussing a big political issue like the old Schleswig-Holstein Question (whatever that was). But 'I have issues with Alex' means 'I think Alex is a twat'. 'I have issues with alcohol' means 'I am a drunk'.

There was a staunch defence of the use of the word 'issues' recently by a columnist in the *Boston Globe*, who pointed out that legal disputes have involved 'issues of fact' – where conflicting parties have opposing statements that need to be debated and verified – since the 14th century. I, for example, may go to court with a neighbour over 'issues' relating to a boundary fence. This, the *Boston Globe* continues, evolved over the centuries to mean in political circles 'important matters to be dealt with' and makes perfect sense as an alternative word to 'problem'.

Well, frankly, I don't care what the technical derivation of 'issues' is, but as it happens the *Boston Globe* has just given me another reason to hate it: the Law. Why should we allow the Law to influence how we speak as well as almost every other aspect of our lives? Stupid laws on health and safety now govern everything from whether a football match goes ahead if it's a bit snowy, in case fans are injured on the way to the ground and one of them sues the football club, to whether I am allowed to stand on a chair in my office to reach a DVD without wearing a fluorescent bib. Other laws forbid people to express their disapproval of someone else's behaviour by tutting at them; a man was fined for sending a jokey text message about blowing up an airport; science journalists are sued under libel laws that restrict the use of scientific data to disprove bogus medical claims; and a man was once arrested for calling a police horse 'gay' on the grounds that 'his remarks were deemed likely to cause harassment, alarm or distress'. So bollocks to the Law and all its works and all its empty promises and if that includes any technical justification for the use of the word 'issues' then so much the better.

Goddess

Like the inner diva, the 'goddess' within is something ladies are frequently encouraged to release by nutty New Age therapists and self-help gurus.

'Goddess' is a much overused term now, and, in a culture like ours where superlatives and hyperbole are so clapped out they could be hosting a game show on Channel 4, it's a way of elevating a celebrity to an even higher status than Superwoman, Überwoman or even National Treasure. A 'goddess' can be a woman merely well known in her field, who has just happened to appear at a cashpoint in time for the *Heat* magazine photographer to snap her for the inevitable caption: 'Pop goddess Katy Perry strapped for cash as she pops to her local Greggs to pick up a couple of vanilla slices'.

And of course we have Nigella Lawson, the 'domestic goddess'. This is the person upon whom the term 'goddess' now resides most comfortably, for all the morons who use it.

Nigella is the posh woman who grins weirdly and wobbles her head a lot while cooking. All right, she's also the one with the massive arse, sorry, did I say arse? I meant knockers. Anyway, she is somehow divinely miraculous for being a) beautiful and b) able to cook, and she manages to cram all that into her busy lifestyle and still hold down her job, which involves, er, looking good and cooking. If she ran a minicab business or designed and built the Dyson Airblade under a pseudonym and still looked good and cooked beautiful food, then I would think – yes, OK, she's put a shift in there. But she's a 'goddess' for being able to do all the things she's famous for doing. It's a bit like the New Year's Honours List that gives people awards for doing what they do for a living anyway.

To be fair to Nigella, she pretty much coined the term 'domestic goddess' herself as the title of a book about baking and being a bit motherly (a nod to the domestic, or hearth, goddesses of Roman mythology who guard the home and everyone in it).

I'm sure she'd be the first to admit that the 'goddess' thing is total bollocks, as she clearly has a sense of humour. All the fellating of chocolate fingers in a negligee at the end of the show is, you might say, tongue in cheek, much like everything else on the programme. She can't possibly live in that flat – there's not enough room to swing Charles Saatchi's wallet – and now she is obliged to get a taxi to her local 7–11 (the look on the driver's face says: 'You've never spoken to me before in your life') because it emerged the BBC were paying people to sit on the bus with her while they filmed her using public transport. I'm not entirely sure that the 'friends' who come round to Nigella's pad to sample her ambrosia are all genuine, either. But the book sales and the popularity of her TV series declare that it must indeed be ambrosia and she can no doubt afford to bathe in asses' milk, so that's good enough justification for today's culture that she *must* be a 'goddess'.

Nigella has certainly set unusual standards for modern female divinity – riches, talent, beauty, knockers and a wobbly head – compared to the days when all a woman needed to become a 'goddess' was to appear in half a dozen classic movies with Clark Gable or Humphrey Bogart.

Any Time Soon

● ●

This is probably the very combination of words that made me want to write a book about twat-speak in the first place. It has all the qualities for a thoroughly loathsome phrase.

1. It's an Americanism that even many Americans can't bear.

2. It's meaningless and wastes more time to say than the word it replaces.
3. It has nothing to do with the evolution of language but everything to do with fashion.
4. It's used, and proliferated by, journalists and TV presenters who, almost by definition, should know better.

You can see how it would originate in America. It has an informal familiar tone with an impatient quality about it, a bit like another pet hate of mine 'the best just got better'. 'Any time soon' also arrogantly suggests that whoever is saying it is totally in control of all possible situations, has arrived at an appointed venue ages before anyone else and has a calendar, a watch and timetables of all incoming flights and train arrivals. 'Don't expect them to arrive any time soon, because, believe me, I know and I won't hold my breath.' Maybe that is why journalists use it with such nauseating frequency – 'I'm totally across this story, so don't expect a deal on climate change/a U-turn on government policy any time soon.'

But you would think that journalists who pride themselves on their economical use of language would reject a phrase like this out of hand, because it's so wasteful. 'Any time soon' just means 'soon'. Even though it is an Americanism it sounds

so inelegant even out of an American mouth and there are dozens of chatrooms and forums in the US where it appears near the top of their most hated phrases. From a British person it is unforgivable, elbowing out the obvious 'in the near future', which may take slightly longer to say but what's one syllable compared to the loss of your self-respect? From a British person's mouth it screams, 'I watch too many American TV dramas.'

To be fair to print journalists, 'ATS' (I can't even stand to write it out in full any more) appears far less frequently in newspapers. Presumably the in-house style guides are stamping it out as they did with phrases like 'brown is the new black' once *Private Eye*'s 'Neophiliacs' column had begun pillorying lazy hacks over it. Phrases like this spread among journalists like a brand-new fashion trend, e.g. when Matt, Luke and Ken from Bros started wearing Grolsch bottle tops on their shoes, or much more recently like the 'metrosexual scarf' fad. This trend became such a conscious fashion statement that even the *Daily Telegraph* picked up on it. It was a different way some men (i.e. David Beckham) chose to wear their scarves to show they were more in touch with their feminine side and more than just thuggish footballers. You know what I mean – it was *de rigueur* for all female BBC reporters at one time but on most men it just looks, well, gay. The traditional man's scarf was worn either just hung around the neck under an overcoat or knotted in the football fan-style. Clearly, one day, a male reporter, probably Justin Webb (though I'm not casting any doubts on his sexuality), started tying it another way. Next thing you know they're all doing it and now you can't buy a scarf less than four feet long and more than three inches wide, so the only way to tie it is in the metrosexual manner.

But Justin Webb, Fergus Walsh, Hugh Pym, Damian Grammaticas and Rajesh Mirchandani are not metrosexual clotheshorses, they are serious journalists. Furthermore, they are BBC journalists covering floods in Doncaster, and the closure of pubs in Merthyr Tydfil, they are not covering the impeachment of Nixon or crossing swords with Josiah Bartlett of *The West Wing*.

I have become so sensitised to 'ATS' that I can almost feel it coming as the reporter laboriously builds up to the end of their report. I know people allergic to nuts and pulses who come out in lumpy red blotches if someone so much as waves a lentil at them. In the same way, as I sense the *10 O' Clock News* report on a rise in petrol prices is nearing the two-minute mark, I begin to dig my fingernails into the palms of my hands, grit my teeth and double up into the foetal position on the sofa. In fact, I'm almost longing for the vile utterance so that I can relieve myself with an almost primal scream: '... fuel prices may have stabilised for now but don't expect them to fall ANY TIME SOON.' AAAAARRRRGGGGGHHHHH!

National Treasure

This one is slightly different from most of the words and phrases in this book as it's not a neologism or an Americanism; it has been around for decades, maybe hundreds of years, but has recently fallen into severe overuse. 'National treasures' are popping up everywhere – Delia Smith, Terry Wogan, Michael Palin, Dame Judi Dench, Stephen Fry, Sir David Attenborough, even Johnny Rotten have all been given the accolade by some magazine, TV programme or other, and journalists of all descriptions are becoming increasingly eager to slap the equivalent of a blue plaque onto anyone who's been on the television for more than 20 years and isn't dead yet.

Recently, the *Sunday Telegraph* in conjunction with the British Library ran a poll to list the nation's 'national treasures', claiming that heroes and legends were ten-a-penny these days. Well, all that happened is that another handy list was generated so we could all go 'yes, quite right' or 'not that bloody woman', just as we would at the New Year's Honours List or *Today*'s Personality of the Year or the British Comedy Awards. 'National treasure', like 'hero' or 'legend', is just another phrase that allows you to make a pointless list and print pictures of famous people.

'National treasure' status is supposed to signify that something is a shared cultural asset of The People. The concept of a 'national treasure' was one that could be saved for the nation, like a Turner painting. The rot set in with the President of Brazil deciding in 1962 that Pele should be declared a 'national treasure' and not allowed to leave the country to play football for anyone else. This was a fair attempt to prevent the big-money clubs like Real Madrid and Manchester United effectively stealing players from their home towns, but it put the idea into people's heads that they had a new label to stick on celebrities. And so, many years later, we had the sight of Helen Mirren being declared a 'national treasure' on *The Parkinson Show* simply because she'd been drooled over as a guest by Parky so many times before that he'd run out of all the 'byooootiful', 'glamrus' and 'every man's fantasy' type of introductions and had to think of something new and even further over-the-top.

There's no blame attached to those nominated. In fact, they all seem to feel as uncomfortable as I do with the accolade. Recently, *The One Show* – TV's equivalent of a branch of Argos – spent a good deal of time and money sending a reporter all over Britain to ask 'why people like Stephen Fry' so that they could prove to his face – he was cringing in the studio at the time – that he is a 'national treasure'. He was utterly and quite convincingly mortified and even he – even Stephen, the Grand Imperial Wizard and Great Sage of our Age, the fount of all knowledge and pink-bloody-fluffiness – had no idea what it meant.

Season

· ·

How often have you heard someone say 'I really enjoyed Season 3 of *The Wire*'? Maybe not very often at all, as *The Wire* has only ever been seen by a handful of southern media wankers. Being one of those wankers, I am considerably more annoyed by the replacement of the word 'series' than by yet another discussion about a very good, but not great, American TV programme. (Why don't people ever discuss *I, Claudius* or *Tinker, Tailor, Soldier, Spy* at these 'water cooler' moments?)

'Season' is an Americanism, like 'Monday thru Friday', 'different than', 'semester' and 'dime store'. There is absolutely no justification for the word 'season' to come out of a British person's mouth unless he is discussing the climate, football or whether there is too much salt in the mashed potatoes. Some linguistic liberals claim that it's acceptable to say 'season' if you have the DVD of a programme and it says 'season three' on it. I don't think so. For instance, if you'd bought *The Rights of Man* by Thomas Paine, would you say, 'I'm really looking forward to getting home and reading "Part the First – being an answer to Mr Burke's attack on the French Revolution"'? No, you wouldn't, and more importantly nor would an American.

TV nerds who frequent online forums like digitalspy and

notbbc are more than happy to use 'season' because they think the American terminology is superior – 'series' is the actual show, e.g. *The Wire*, and 'season' is the run of episodes (I had to try really hard not to write 'programme' and 'series' there). But this is because the Americans have only one 'season' of about 22 episodes a year, which is why it's called a bloody season in the first place! The clue is in the name! It comes around in the autumn (or fall, as we don't say) after Pilot Season in the early part of the year and production in spring/summer. It's geared entirely to the accounting needs of the big TV networks and production companies and so they can show the programmes – dammit, yes, the programmes – to the advertisers to see if they'll spend any cash in the breaks around them. It's not for the viewers' edification or because they love giving us series with long and involving story arcs, so there is every reason to shun their stupid terminology.

We gave the Americans television and, although they have now overtaken us in sheer quality on some of the cable channels (HBO being the prime example), there's no reason we should allow them and their accounts departments to dictate the overall culture of the English language or any other aspect of the television business. What's next? Are UK broadcasters going to follow in their footsteps and allow twelve-minute advertising breaks and product placement?*

---

*Yes, of course.

Hold Your Hands Up

This phrase is not to be confused with 'put your hands in the air' as favoured by the many DJs of Europe's hottest raveclubbing, disco nitespots. It's in fact much closer to the old injunction issued by heavily armed cowpokes such as Billy the Kid and Wyatt Earp, although it's now less a term for surrender as an admission of responsibility. Apparently, it's a big man who can 'hold his hands up' and say 'My bad' (although if he actually says 'My bad' it's perfectly OK to shoot him). See 'My Bad' on p. 106.

By 'holding your hands up' you can take things on board, accept the blame and 'move forward'. The term's modern usage appears to originate in the game of football, where you might have a gormless defender (usually Glen Johnson) passing the ball casually across his own penalty area so the opposition's predatory striker can nick it, saunter round the keeper and tap it in. As his team-mates put their hands to their faces and the fans make their hands into the 'wanker' shape, the defender holds *his* hands up to acknowledge his guilt. 'Moving on' from this is harder than it sounds, as football crowds tend not to forget imbecilic behaviour, despite there being so much of it in the game, and managers tend to offload serially incompetent footballers (a different sort of 'moving on') faster than you can say Titus Bramble.

As we've found so far, if you've been paying attention, the dull world of the boardroom and the office loves to appropriate the language of the sports field to make its life sound more fascinating, completely forgetting that, by the time a phrase has been worked on in a zillion post-match interviews by football managers and players, it's become totally meaningless ('we've set our stall out', anyone?).

To make matters worse, because Lord Sugar of Amstrad, in the early series of *The Apprentice*, was very keen for candidates not to weasel their way out of trouble by blaming others for their own cock-ups, now every one of the nation's business hot-shots is 'holding their hands up' like a classroom of five-year-olds with bladder problems.

An eagerness to see some people accept responsibility and the willingness of other people to do it has spread right throughout our society now and it's become ridiculous on two levels. First is our desperate need to have someone own up for everything, even when there is no real culprit. Last year the Scottish Transport Minister Stewart Stevenson had to resign when drivers, who had been warned not to travel, got stuck in the snow. So we are asking people to take the blame for everyone else's inability to cope with the weather now? Second, so many apologies are demanded and so many people are holding their hands up and apologising that the apology has become either totally meaningless or just like paying a toll on a motorway. Around the anniversary of the abolition of the slave trade, Tony Blair apologised for it all himself; apologised for something which ended *200 years* before he was born and that he couldn't possibly have done anything about. And in 2010, Business Secretary Vince Cable, having seriously gaffed over his dealings with Rupert Murdoch, should have been sacked but was saved by apologising. He apologised for saying something that he absolutely meant when he said it (and almost certainly still believes now) and the prime minister urged everyone to 'move on – he's embarrassed and he's apologised. That should be the end of it.' It may have been the end of that particular blunder, but it certainly wasn't the last time a Lib Dem had to hold his hands up.

Smashed It

● ●

Ah! We're back to the baseball stadium, where people 'step up to the plate', again. Is it Wrigley Field? Fenway Park? Yankee Stadium? The Little League game in your backyard, perhaps? No, actually, we're in a dull, dismal bit of Little England again; probably the head office of a telecommunications company just off the A14, and somebody has just had a great meeting, in which the words 'moving forward' were probably used. Some bloke called Andy has had his plans approved and afterwards he high-fives his mate Steve, who tells him he 'smashed it out of the park'. It could be even worse. We might be at the Fountain TV studios in Wembley, where Simon Cowell's annual tribute to the Nuremburg Rally, *The X Factor*, is taking place. Some warbly voiced, wobbly-headed teenager from Runcorn has just delivered a dreadful version of a soft-rock classic in a totally unsuitable R'n'B style; the lobotomised crowd are whooping, cheering and applauding like loons and Cheryl Cole trills over the racket – 'Yoo oar a stoar! Yoo reely oar! Yerv toe'allee smashed it!'

The two-hundred-mile journey down the M1 to North London is symbolic of the great cultural divide between the North and the South of England, where people stopped saying the 'out of the park' bit years ago, especially on sophisticated shows like *The X Factor*. Now your average M25 moron is more likely to say simply 'smacked it'. I'm told this could either be a reference to drugs or to the sound of high-fives or the up-down slapping of palms people engage in at moments of triumph, although even that behaviour has been replaced by the ridiculous buffeting of chests by jubilant male tossers or 'fist bumps' – the newest US trend to reach our shores.

I wonder if people in the UK who use the phrase have ever been to a baseball game or seen a home run? Of all the ridiculous American sports it's by far the best; to see someone smash a baseball out of the park and watch the leather ball rising higher and higher, past your seat in row Z, is to recognise quite a sporting achievement. Impressing the guys in sales or murdering a song live on television doesn't even come close.

As a footnote to this entry, a very peculiar media event took place in early 2011, which threw a whole new light on the meaning of the phrase 'smashed it'. It was the public defenestration of football pundits Andy Gray and Richard Keys from Sky Sports. The initial furore was over the pair's comments about the ability of a woman, specifically a Premier League lineswoman (if I'm allowed to say that), to understand the offside rule. Once Sky realised that the national mood was turning against their star names they hung them out to dry by releasing 'off-air' recordings of both men making even more sexist remarks. Andy Gray's was a rudimentary mime that would have passed without comment in a Benny Hill sketch decades earlier, but Richard Keys broke new ground when discussing an attractive woman who, it turned out, had been a one-time conquest of Sky Sports' resident handsome dimwit Jamie Redknapp.

'Did you smash it?' asked Keys, adding, 'Mind you, that's a stupid question. If you were anywhere near it, you'd definitely smash it.'

Was Richard suggesting that Jamie Redknapp was prone to bouts of domestic violence? No – because Richard Keys, being one of Britain's coolest men (he got rid of his mullet really early on in the 90s), was using 'smash it' in the ultra-cutting-edge sense of 'having sex with her', as he immediately went on to illuminate: *'Go round any night of the week and find Redknapp hanging out of the back of it.'*

This is almost certainly the first time anyone had used the phrase 'smash it' in this way. There is much talk about language developing slowly over long periods of time, but I think we can all count ourselves as privileged to witness the very moment when our mother tongue took such an evolutionary leap – backwards by about 40 years.

Go-To Guy

'He's your go-to guy' is now casually tossed off in media circles so frequently that it's become a daily crime that very often goes unremarked upon, like a drive-by shooting in Manchester.

This expression has been stolen from basketball – one of the most pointless and stupid non-sports ever invented. Squeaking shoes; big, daft baggy shorts; random shouting; a lot of pushing; 'travelling'; and then someone scores and the other team goes down the other end and does the same and it goes on and on for what seems like weeks. I can grimly remember those awful games lessons in the gloomy school gym, when we were forced to play basketball in the fading light of a wintry afternoon: about a dozen, short-arsed, skinny white kids, flapping and shrieking as we took it in turns to miss a hoop which seemed to be floating in space, half a mile above us.

Anyway, as I understand it, a 'go-to guy' is someone you would automatically trust to solve a problem or get something done in a given situation, like put the basketball in the basket, although I thought everyone on a basketball team was supposed to do that.

How did such an ugly phrase spread so quickly? Never being a fan of the word 'guy' in the first place (I still wince a little when children try to get everyone's attention by shouting 'guys!'), I can't imagine what would drive me to jam it together with two other ill-suited words and say 'go-to guy', when what I meant was 'expert'. Or 'he's really good at that'.

I know professional gag-writers who use the phrase 'go to' when writing a joke that requires a widely recognised example of a particular behaviour or attribute to make the punchline work. So, for a joke about something costing a ridiculous amount of money, the gag-writer normally refers to a latte from Starbucks, or a Duchy of Cornwall biscuit, as an effective 'go to' comparison. Or if it's a drunk joke, the 'go to' is now probably Paul Gascoigne, when once it was Oliver Reed and before that George Brown. Or – we may as well observe the rule of three if we're talking about gag-writing – if an unreliable airline is needed, Aeroflot has now replaced Dan-Air. But no self-respecting gag-writer, or professional writer of any kind, would knowingly refer to someone as a 'go-to guy'.

To my horror, most of the examples I found on the internet are of people using it to describe themselves: someone called Nick Macchiarella claims on his website that he is 'your go-to guy ... for providing creative solutions for business clientele'.

Another man called Arnold Andersen writes: 'From now on, consider me your go-to guy for solving debt, credit and financial problems.'

consider me your go-to guy for solving debt, credit and financial problems.'

But my favourite claim comes from this chap:

Andre Mertz is The Go-To Guy! and also the founder of Go-To Guy! Enterprises.

I shouldn't really do this but, if you do know where the Go-To Guy's offices are, why don't you go to him and shove an envelope full of macaroni cheese through the letterbox? But attach a note with a Mr Hal Humberton's number on it, because on his website he describes himself as 'the go-to guy for all your carpet cleaning solutions'.

My Bad

This is said to have originated from street basketball. Players used it when they made a bad pass and wanted to take responsibility. And so yet another basketball term spreads to England and multiplies. Why are we adopting the language of basketball? I know that a few people play the game in this popularity and cultural influence in Britain but people don't shout 'Man on! Back door! Turn and face!' to each other in the office.

Fair enough, 'my bad' is quick to say and in a speedy game of basketball who cares if it's ungrammatical? Although, when I was a kid, if I was playing any kind of game in the playground and I made a mistake, 'sorry' was just as quick to say and 'soz' was even better. Nevertheless, why would you go around saying 'my bad' in normal conversation? 'I've just deleted an entire year's worth of immigration statistics. My bad.' It sounds a bit, well, ignorant.

'Only to a racist', say some linguistic experts. 'My bad' is, according to them, a perfectly valid dialect called 'African American Vernacular English' and, just as many people suffer racial prejudice, 'so they also suffer dialect prejudice'. Not being a racist, I wouldn't call it dialect prejudice, I'd call it ignorance prejudice.

Of course, everyone who uses 'my bad' knows it's not grammatically correct. The education of ethnic minorities has been neglected by governments over the decades but it is not so poor that simple English has been abandoned. 'My bad' is used for effect. Defiant ignorance is used by many people, black and white, to assert their identity, particularly in America. Tea Party rednecks and Sarah Palin's acolytes wilfully parade their lack of sophistication in the face of liberal intellectuals with their posters proclaiming slogans like 'Obama Bin Lyin''.

But adopting someone else's defiant ignorance for yourself is just plain embarrassing to you and patronising to them. Though not quite as bad as the white people who say 'ma nigger', those just plain embarrassing to you and patronising to them. Though not quite as bad as the white people who say 'ma nigger', those who say 'my bad' are right up there in the league of twattery. The phrase gained currency among the white middle classes through the film *Clueless*, in which a stupid white high-school girl carelessly calls it out, when her reckless driving almost kills someone. And from there it has derived its newer meaning: nothing. It's not really an apology at all; it means 'I know it was my fault but I don't care'.

No-Brainer

• •

I can see the appeal of this – it's jokey and self-explanatory and pleasingly autological in that, as a phrase, it has clearly had no thought applied to its construction; it sounds like the person saying it is lacking a fully functioning brain.

Ironically, the trouble with 'no-brainer' is that people use it now without thinking at all. It's applied to certain situations or decisions which do actually require some thought and the people who utter it should think twice before doing so. Like a lot of these wilfully dumb expressions, it's used by people who should know better; people who write for a living. A political correspondent for the *Guardian* newspaper for example, in the aftermath of the 2010 general election, wrote that 'the Lib Dems' choice of coalition partner is a no-brainer'; he went on to explain that if it came down to a choice between the Tories and Labour then Labour were the obvious, the natural choice. Of course, this was not a no-brainer on so many levels that it's laughable. Modern journalists do love to pep up their pieces with attention-grabbing language and fashionable or hip turns of phrase. The journalist in this case could have written 'For the Lib Dems, Labour as a coalition partner seems, on the face of it, to be an obvious choice.' This would have been

a) accurate at the time and b) still accurate three days later when the Tories announced the Lib Dems would be propping them up in government (and taking the blame for all the bad stuff).

Of course, journalists are not encouraged by their editors to be circumspect, but to report something inaccurately for the sake of crowbarring in a certain turn of phrase is bewildering. Just as primary school children are encouraged by their teachers to use lots of 'wow' words in their writing (i.e. not just repeating the word 'nice' for everything), it means that they start looking for superlatives, exaggerations and hyperbole instead of explaining what's actually going on. In neither case is it very helpful, which I would have thought was so obvious it requires no thought at all.

Cool/Wicked

● ●

Who would have thought that people would still be saying 'cool' and 'wicked' decades after The Fonz and Lenny Henry's Delbert Wilkins? Of the two, 'cool' has enjoyed the most mixed fortunes, with many a resurgence and decline over the last 70 years. In the late 1970s and early 80s, it was decidedly uncool to say 'cool' (unless you were The Fonz) but 30 years before that it was almost compulsory and often accompanied by 'Daddio'. I can't really pinpoint when it came back – with Britpop, maybe? New Labour's use of 'Cool Britannia' should have been the kiss of death for the word but it seems to have influenced a generation of young people, now in their thirties, who say 'cool' as a kind of reflex action, as if they were blinking.

Of course, not everyone who says 'cool' will go deeper into forbidden territory and say 'cool beans'. These people are a bit like lepers ringing a bell warning you not to talk to them – 'Cool beans! Unclean! Cool Beans! Unclean!'

That same Britpop generation and their younger siblings will also happily come out with 'wicked' as though Delbert Wilkins had never existed. Along with Old Man Deakus and JYTV's Joshua Yarlog, Delbert may well give the lie to the old 'Lenny Henry isn't funny' jibe, but his greatest crime is to have given legitimacy to the work 'wicked'. Delbert was clearly mocking the use of it but everybody loved it; he said it for a laugh and then it stuck. Disappointingly, some other far superior catchphrases have not stood the test of time like 'wazzuuuup' and 'Magic, our Maurice'.*

There seems to be no way to stop the spread of 'cool' and 'wicked'. Even the wife of the future king, Camilla Parker Bowles, used 'wicked' to describe the news of her stepson's engagement. We will have to place all our hope in the young; that, with their limitless capacity to invent annoying words, they will come up with the 'cool/wicked' killer. One youth told me that 'book' is actually the new 'cool' because that's what 'cool' gives you when typing a predictive text message. Nice try, kid, but I'm afraid the growing numbers of people 'shopping' iPhone (see next entry) will gradually render even text language obsolete.

*Selwyn Froggitt.

Shop/Store

There are so many problems with this one, I'm not sure where to begin.

Let's start with the obvious: a shop is where you buy things and a store is where you store things, like a grain store or, if there are any Americans reading, an ammunition store. So you buy things in a shop and you retrieve things from a store. You do not 'shop' a shop and you certainly do not 'shop' a store. Or do you? Are there really people out there who say, 'I'm just going to shop the Sainsbury's store'? I sincerely hope not but I fear that, if we are not vigilant, the 'store shoppers' will overwhelm us like the vegetable pods in *Invasion of the Body Snatchers*.

This is far from being yet another gripe about nouns being turned into verbs, although personally I will complain about that until the cows re-shed. No, the 'shop/store' problem is actually the tip of a massive global iceberg called Apple. The original, overfamiliar injunction on their website to 'shop the store' (and add to the several hundred billion dollars a second that they make) has been replaced now by the even more alarming Shop Mac, Shop iPod, Shop iPhone, Shop iPad buttons at www.apple.com. This is Orwell's nightmare of doublespeak coming true, and when they put up 'Shop App Store' I'll know the cretinisation of civilisation is complete.

I say all this as a self-confessed Apple imbecile. I can't help but fall for the very things for which they have carefully planned for me to fall. White plastic, brushed steel, rubberised buttons, rounded edges – they know I want them all. They have even told me quite openly that they are going to fool me and dupe me and rip me off and I've happily bought the ticket for the Bunco Booth. Their advertising and product design is so obviously targeted that it's like being at a Derren Brown performance, in which he tells you you're going to be hypnotised into thinking you're Dr Magdi Yacoub's anaesthetist and, resist though you may, by the end of the evening, you're performing a heart, liver and lung transplant. So, even though I know that an iPad is just an iPod Touch which is too big to fit into my pocket, I will still stump up the ridiculous £490 for it, like a twat.

I thank the Lord for the existence of Theshopstore.co.uk. Yes, it really does exist. It not only stocks all the stuff you need if you are opening a shop – tills, shelves, baskets, counterfeit note detectors etc., but its name also points out the difference between the two words and how they should be used. It's just a shame that they have to actually sell things and can't just store all the shop equipment in the store because then the linguistic distinction would be crystal clear. Obviously, Theshopshop.co.uk would be a much more accurate British name. I might even consider registering the domain name (if Mark Zuckerberg can trademark the word 'face', why not?) and somehow making it appear as spam on the computer of every person who visits the Apple Store.

Listen Up, People!

What could possibly be wrong with this, I hear you ask? Obviously, I don't object to the word 'people' – it's a handy plural of 'person', and much better than 'persons'. Who in their right mind says 'persons' except the people who write signs for local councils and the police spokesmen on *Crimewatch*?

No, 'people' only becomes a problem – albeit a major one – when preceded by the words 'listen' and 'up', as in: 'Listen up, people!' It's normally accompanied by a couple of vigorous handclaps and said in an open-plan office while rotating the head through 180 degrees as if making a mental note of exactly who is paying attention. It's barely acceptable when the duplicitous CIA director says it in the Command Centre when they are looking for Jason Bourne; it's certainly not acceptable when Trevor the sales director puts down his paper cup by the water cooler and calls for attention from the guys and the ladies in the sales department of Doubleday Windows, Croxteth.

Why on earth can't Trevor slightly raise his voice, possibly tap a glass with a pencil and say, 'Could I have everybody's attention, please'? With the requisite authority in the voice, who on Trevor's sales team could possibly ignore him? No need for any of that 'people' nonsense, as if the speaker has been on a gender awareness course led by David Brent.

'Listen up, people!' also places a huge weight of expectation on what you're about to say. You may as well have a little Napoleonic drummer boy standing next to you to give you a roll just as you're about to speak, or a town crier with a handbell, shouting 'oyez, oyez'.

The trouble is, the sort of idiot who does say 'Listen up, people!' is convinced that what he has to say is important enough to warrant that introduction. It's hard to know how to advise a group of workmates on how to deal with it. The most natural reaction is to bang down the coffee mug on the desk and sigh 'What now?' But I think listening in an overexaggeratedly attentive way with especially bright eyes and lolling tongue, while the master speaks, followed by the saddest look of crushing disappointment when he's finished, is the best recommendation.

You Know What?

●●

This phrase is a close relation of 'Listen up, people!' but it's like a mini drum roll introduction for the moment when you're in a more intimate conversation and you want to give what you're about to say some import. For example: 'You know what? Let him fire me.'

It almost demands that you adopt a tough-guy, bugger-the-consequences, just-you-wait-and-see attitude. 'Maybe it will be an awkward meeting. You know what? I don't care.'

As an original Americanism that would be much more at home on a street corner in Hoboken, it's almost begging to be followed by '… and foidermore'.

My beef with 'You know what?' is that, because it seems to come from the mean streets of New York, it's nearly always a prelude to slightly rude or aggressive behaviour. Serial 'you-know-what-ers' can find that this attitude travels home with them:

'You know what? Don't take the bins out. I'll do it myself. And I'll get my own dinner ready and you can go fuck yourself yadda yadda yadda.'

Imagine how wrong that would sound coming from the mouth of someone from Dudley?

The other problem with 'You know what?' is that people are using it in the most inappropriate circumstances. I recently overheard a mother saying it to her three-year-old: 'You know what? You're still going to nursery whether you're crying or not.'

Of course, by now you may have reached the point in the book where you're beginning to think I am slightly deranged and am now just picking on any combination of words that I don't like the sound of. It's partially true but, although I may be currently out on my own with my 'You know what?' gripe, mark my words, it's spreading.

48

Head-to-Head

● ●

Yes, OK, it's a literal translation of *tête-à-tête*, but actually the rather more gentle 'face-to-face' does that job much better. 'Head-to-head' now no longer conjures up an intimate conversation between two people because, thanks to the hype of Sky Sports with the now long-gone Richard Keys, 'head-to-head' has come to mean a titanic clash between a couple of mediocre football clubs, illustrated by the animated crests of said teams smashing into each other. This takes place halfway into the five-hour build-up on Sky Sports 3 to the 'BIG GAME' between Wigan and Fulham, a game that you couldn't get excited about even if the players were sailing pirate galleons and firing the football out of a cannon. But Richard Keys was always totally energised, whoever was playing – 'Let's have a look at the head-to-head,' he would say as the club crests collided, and then we'd see a list of old scores stretching back a few years. 'Wigan haven't beaten Fulham on their own ground for 72 years,' Richard would intone, with all the portent and foreboding of Nostradamus, 'and that was 1–0 on the first Saturday in February – just like today.' Never were statistics more meaningless. Most of the players on both sides weren't born 20 years ago and they probably can't remember further back than last week. Even if they could, it's completely irrelevant; the result of the same fixture, even if it was two days ago, would have absolutely no bearing on the outcome of a game today. So 'head-to-head' is a feeble attempt to make something sound more exciting than it is. Just like when Bruce Forsyth says 'the bottom two couples will go head-to-head in a dance-off'. It's ballroom dancing, not the end of *Fistful of Dollars*.

The only arena where 'head-to-head' can be accurately applied is the boxing ring, where a couple of Neanderthals will occasionally grind their foreheads together in between trying to knock each other senseless. An appropriately futile exercise for such an empty phrase.

49

Don't Even Go There

This phrase is still much loved by radio presenters and local TV news 'characters' throughout the country. 'Don't even go there' is the sort of thing the regional weatherman says when his banter with the local news anchor has strayed into risqué territory.

> *'You can look forward to a warm front tonight, Judith, and some very damp conditions in the south.'*
> *'Oops. Don't even go there, Andy!'*

It implies that everyone is in on a rather naughty conspiracy together and the joke they can all see coming is so rude it's better left alone. In fact, there is often no dangerous territory at all and only a very po-er Finbarr Saunders joke at the end of it, badly delivered to boot.

'Don't even go there' belongs with the other telltale indicators of a very poor sense of humour such as signs that say 'Congratulations, you are now a certified loony', 'In case of stress, bang head here', anything in Comic Sans, car stickers giving 'the finger' and – the worst of all – pictures of dogs playing pool.

People in this country use 'don't even go there' in a desperate attempt to give their humorous exchanges the sizzle of the urban gays and ghetto queens who originally coined the phrase in the early 90s. It quickly spread among the female participants in *The Jerry Springer Show*, who would often add 'girlfriend' on the end and accompany the phrase with a head-wobble and a double-snap of the fingers. Usually, the warning not to 'go there' was followed by a cat-fight leading to a full-scale brawl in the studio. I think everyone has the duty to encourage the same response to anyone using it nowadays.

Pecs, Abs, Glutes, etc.

Maybe it's unreasonable to object to abbreviated words – they're useful and will always occur – but the familiarity of 'pecs', 'abs' and 'glutes' (to name but a few) with the parts of the body they denote seems to me to be as creepy as calling your parents by their first names. Of course, the obvious parts of the body will be persistently associated with slang but other body parts don't really suit abbreviations. No one would say, 'I've got a canc tume in my liv,' would they?

Abbreviated medical terms are the kind of things overfamiliar medical staff use; the ones who will casually call an old person by their Christian name ('We'll just examine your front bottom, Olive') or, more commonly, people who feel really rather pleased with the condition of their own bodies. 'Yeah, this exercise will really sort my pecs out' – you would never say that if you were a massively overweight, beer-bellied slob with man breasts. (I'm not going to say 'man boobs' or 'moobs' because I would rather die.) You wouldn't even say pectoral muscles, you'd say 'chest'. Equally, you'd refer to your flabby old gut as your stomach, not your 'abdominal core'. But 'glutes' and 'quads' are exactly what that rather cocky personal trainer-type says as he struts around the gym. He should say bottom or buttocks but he's qualified, you see; he knows all the medical terms, and yet there's no way he's got time in his busy schedule to say 'gluteus maximus' so you'll get 'glutes', 'delts' and probably 'quads' (whatever they are) instead.

I understand that the number of personal trainers is increasing (forecast to rise by 20 per cent in the next ten years) as more and more single people spend their money on making themselves more attractive to other single people. But people don't realise the damage that they are doing to themselves and their vocabulary, and before they know it they will have moved on from 'pecs' and 'abs' to using even more terrible words like 'cut', 'ripped' and 'buff', if they haven't already.

Even now the phrase 'upper body strength' appears to have replaced perfectly acceptable words like 'muscular', 'well built' and 'stocky'. This too, like 'abs', 'pecs' and 'glutes', has the whiff of the changing room at a local fitness centre about it. Now hundreds of activities claim that they will boost your upper body strength – archery, yachting, diving, cycling, arm wrestling, origami, yahtzee – when they would once have been said simply to 'keep you fit'. This kind of pseudo-technical jargon is exactly the sort of nonsense Arnie as the Terminator (effectively a personal trainer in leathers) would come out with; rubbish like 'I am a cybernetic organism, living tissue over a metal endoskeleton'.

Arnie himself is actually even less interesting than the Cyberdyne Systems Model 101 character he portrayed – and what has made him like that is too much time spent in a gym working on his 'glutes'.

My Inner ...

The 'inner' *whatever* is assumed to be your true personality; the real you, the self to which you are supposed to be true.

Every day some magazine, newspaper, daytime TV show or other will be encouraging people to release their 'inner' diva. Interestingly, on certain websites, releasing the inner diva can be achieved by 'sexy lingerie for plus-size figures' or 'pole dancing in your own home'. The very thought of it makes me want to release my inner dinner.

In opera terms, a diva is one step away from a prima donna and, as everyone knows, prima donna is just an Italian's way of saying 'pain in the arse'; in fact, it's almost the definition of one. No one, of course, will ever be encouraged to release their 'inner' chartered accountant or their 'inner' telephone salesperson, because the 'inner' thing you're supposed to release is nearly always either arrogant, self-centred or attention-grabbing: the 'inner' rock chick, catwalk model or vamp. And it's almost certainly going to be distasteful to everyone else. Maybe it's 'inner', locked away or hidden because you realised early on in life that it was unattractive or objectionable. Should I release my 'inner' racist? Best not. Did it help Fred West to grow spiritually to release his 'inner' psychotic murderer? I don't think so.

To Podium/Medal

We have been in the gruesome territory of anthimeria* before: using one type of word to do another type's job – the linguistic equivalent of scab labour. Two of the most nauseating examples surfaced in the Beijing (is 'Peking' racist?) Olympics of 2008. Great Britain – let's not mention Team GB again – won more medals than they'd won for a hundred years, but the athletes didn't see it that way. According to them, they 'medalled' or occasionally 'podiumed'. Who told them to say this? Was it their coaches who were effectively brainwashing them all as they pursued their dream? I don't remember Geoff Capes or Alan Minter or Brendan Foster talking about achieving goals and pursuing dreams when they were Olympians. They trained hard and tried their best to, what they quaintly used to call, 'win'. I'd rather we came bottom of the medals table than hear about any more of our athletes 'podiuming' or 'medalling'.

Even the official Olympic website refers to 'the medalled athletes at the last Olympics', so what hope is there for us of escaping it? I suppose the lesson here is that we shouldn't look to official sporting bodies for hope of any kind. Until recently, the International Olympic Committee was a byword for corruption, dodgy deals and

---

*Come on, keep up.

poor standards – obviously, FIFA now stands in a league of its own in that regard.

Etymology anoraks observe that 'podiumed' dates back to the Olympics of the early 1960s – and 'medalled' is even traceable to Victorian times. I don't care how far back they can trace it. Clearly, in Victorian times and even in the 60s there were certain standards which ensured that the casual use of these types of words was stamped out. The only reason people say it now is because some snowboarding pillocks at the winter Olympics in 1998 started using it and vocabulary standards have slipped so much in the last 20 years that, rather than take the normal course of action and do the opposite of whatever a snowboarder does, other athletes and, worst of all, seasoned professional journalists like Adrian Chiles and Clare Balding started saying it, too.

Why should the BBC – never mind international sportsmen, some of whom actually receive knighthoods (albeit for riding a bike or rowing in a straight line) – feel the need to dumb down their vocabulary to the level of snowboarders? So they can seem more 'in touch' with the ordinary viewer, who never has and probably never will go goofy-footed into a half-pipe. I don't recall the original Reithian motto of the BBC being 'Nation shall speak like an arse unto nation'.

Fail!

● ●

As far back as 1998* 'Fail!' entered the vocabulary of gaming addicts and internet nerds and as meaningless slang it was surely going to fall out of fashion as quickly as 'crucial' or 'suss' (or any of the other daft expressions kids used back then) until it was picked up by dunderheads who write blogs and post video comments on YouTube. 'Fail!' is normally typed rather than spoken but you can just imagine it being blurted out by dorks who model themselves on Chris from *Family Guy*, whenever they see any activity that has the slightest hint of potential embarrassment – 'durrr fail!!' Most recently, and more widely, the word 'Epic' has been added to increase the implied ridicule and at the same time compound the grammatical error.

'Fail', or 'epic fail', basically translates as 'ner ner ni ner ner' (or for slightly younger readers 'Doh') but it allows the kids who use it to feel a bit cooler and more grown up than that, which is sad because it's really quite childish in itself. But let the kids have their silly little words. It's the adults who use it that we have to worry about. The success of FAILblog online, which basically

*From the Japanese video game Blazing Star in which the screen declared to a loser: 'You fail it!'

displays pictures of stuff not working properly with 'FAIL!' stamped on it in big red letters, has spread 'Fail!' to a wider audience than just kids and it's turning into as annoying a soundtrack to the decade as 'Quack Quack Oops!' did in the 70s. There is in the humour of Dave Lee Travis, the Hairy Cornflake, something eerily similar to the nerdy quality of the people who say 'FAIL!', as you would discover if you typed 'Quack Quack Oops' into YouTube and had a look at the videos alongside it. And, like everyone who thinks they are funnier than they are, they never know when to stop. I'm waiting for the day when I announce to the office that I've just had my results back from the doctor and I've only got six months to live, and the work-experience lad shouts 'Epic Fail!' at me.

Kick Back

I'm not quite sure exactly which activity 'kick back' is referring to. Is it swimming on your back in a pool or reclining on one of those plastic outdoor loungers or on an electronic easy chair? Whichever it is, I don't like it. It's a word for the ambitiously idle. I don't claim to be an industrious or lively person but at least

I know how to do nothing properly and unimaginatively: slumped sideways on a sofa reading a book or watching a BBC4 documentary about Thin Lizzy. There's something studied about 'kick back' – someone is deliberately trying to make the most of an expensive holiday or they are obeying a magazine journalist's instructions on the fashionable way to take it easy. 'Kick back' is now an obligatory term in any puff piece of journalism or advertising copy revolving around music compilations, a holiday destination or a chocolate product.

Here's an ad for a drinking-chocolate product called Divine.

Kick Back with Divine
£10.00
Enjoy an indulgent evening in with a warm mug of delicious
Divine Hot Chocolate in a beautiful Divine Mug.

It's ten quid for a tub of drinking chocolate in a free mug but by 'kicking back' you somehow turn it into an indulgent, semi-sexual experience. If the copywriter had more space, I guarantee they'd have stuck in a 'pamper yourself' somewhere too.

You'll also find 'kick back' on the sleeve of (what used to be called) music to chill out to. There are people out there who are actually on a mission to find it; here's an online request from a man called Dundas: 'Lookin' for music I can kick back to while I blaze this blunt'.

He appears to want to set fire to an unsharpened pencil but if that's how he relaxes then fine. Several people chipped in with recommendations for Dundas, all of them, naturally, shit. He could have sorted himself out by purchasing 'Music to Kick

Back to on Amazon', which includes several tracks by Jack Johnson, the annoying surf-dude man. It strikes me that, if you wanted to save yourself a lot of time and disappointment from listening to really *really* terrible music, you should just search for 'music to kick back to' and you can safely strike off everything that Google serves you. I would go so far as to recommend the same course of action for holiday destinations. When I Googled 'kick-back holidays' I got Thailand, Mykonos, Maldives, Kerala, Goa. Which shows the system works, because I'd ruled them all out years ago (*Can't Be Arsed*, still excellent value at £9.99).

Reach Out

Not wishing to belittle the emotional fragility of anyone who calls the Samaritans or a priest or a close friend in times of need, I'll accept the use of 'reaching out', as articulated in the magnificent Four Tops single 'Reach Out (I'll Be There)'. In this excusable use of the phrase, occurring mainly in the 1950s and 1960s, it is the needy, vulnerable person who is 'reaching out' to someone else. They are the ones in trouble but they are taking it upon themselves to do something about it. In a religious context, it's connected to the idea of salvation, which you have to want for yourself to achieve it.

The religious and the spiritual began to blend into the New Age and the nonsensical in the 1970s and 1980s, and phrases like 'reach out' tended to have more to do with less vital needs such as hugging than communicating with one another. Now we have websites like Reaching Out Together. It's an email chatroom and online meeting place that carries the motto:

Life is not about waiting for the storm to pass; it is about learning to dance in the rain.

I have said my piece about dancing in the rain (*Can't Be Arsed,* etc.) and its casual use here tells you all you need to know about the kind of people who are Reaching Out Together across cyberspace. I fervently hope they make contact with someone then they'll be less likely to approach me.

You get a sense of just how pathetic a species we are becoming when you realise that in certain parts of America – the parts which have the most influence on the rest of the English-speaking world – to 'reach out' to someone now means to ring them up or just attempt to talk to them. I'm sure this has its origins in the world of show business, where I discovered recently that, if a producer is going to make a call to an agent to book an artiste, he says he is going to 'reach out' to them. What a turnaround from the earlier sense of 'need' implicit in that spiritual reaching out, to the neediness of certain members of the 'talent community' (as it's called) to whom you have to 'reach out' and practically beg to accept huge amounts of money to do a bit of acting.

56

From the Get-Go

● ●

You know someone has been spending too long in the United States – or is basically just a twat – if they start saying 'From the get-go'. My boss says it a lot but, thankfully, I happen to know he is well travelled.

'From the get-go' is another Americanism that isn't any quicker to say than the word it's replacing; 'from the start' is actually one syllable shorter.

Some think the phrase is a shortened, snappier version of 'get up and go' or even 'get ready, set, go!' But that's hardly acceptable, is it? Taking a few words out to shorten a sentence and making it childishly ungrammatical at the same time? Although I just did that, sort of.

The real kiss of death for 'from the get-go' is the fact that you'll find it's usually used by geeks and nerds to make their hugely uninteresting work sound exciting, as if they've found oil on the moon. And that uninteresting work is nearly always something to do with IT. Here are some Google search results for 'get-go'. As the get go-ers might say, check these out:

'Front-end optimization from the get-go!'
(Ooh, that sounds fun! Oh, it's about redesigning a website)

'Preventing usability problems from the get-go.'
(Hmm, that's about designing an air-travel booking form)

'How to install Wordpress with decent security from the get-go.'
(Yes, shazzam! There's your Wordpress with decent security
installed in the blink of an eye. Job done!)

I don't want any IT people out there to think I'm getting at them
or that I have anything personal against the IT people I work
with. I'm just curious as to why so much of the new twat-speak
has its origins among, or is spread around by, IT people. Is it
because they already work in a different language from the rest
of us on a day-to-day basis to talk to computers? (Do they still
have BASIC?) It's true that, throughout its history, the English
language has had many great and powerful influences on its
development – the Greeks, the Romans, the French, the
Germans, revolutionary politics, the age of steam, a century of
warfare. But Dave from IT?

57

Happy Bunny

●●

This most commonly occurs in the negative statement 'not a happy bunny'. It's the sort of thing someone in an office who prides themselves on not losing their cool and remaining 'professional' in trying circumstances will say. According to them, that person who is not a 'happy bunny' has also at one time thrown his 'toys out of the pram' and failed to get all his 'ducks in a row'. It's a phrase for people who are obviously repressing their anger and being passive-aggressive. They want you to know they are pissed off, but in a cute cuddly way. It belongs on a poster to be stuck up by the coffee machine along with 'Are we having fun yet?', 'It takes fewer muscles to frown than to smile' and 'Cheer up, it might never happen'.

Searching for uses of 'happy bunny' on the internet (the source of most research these days, academic or not), I made two interesting discoveries. The first was 'It's Happy Bunny' – a multimillion-dollar marketing phenomenon based on a cute, smiling cartoon rabbit with an abusive phrase underneath it like 'Hi there, shit for brains'. There appear to be a billion variations on this theme, emblazoned on merchandise as varied as rucksacks, pencil cases, T-shirts and even baby grows ('I just shat myself, deal with it'*). Sometimes you come across a funny one and then you hate yourself for laughing at it.

I also discovered a website called www.realsimplepeople.com (motto – 'Keeping Life Simple') where they report that there are seven words that can stop you from being a 'happy bunny'. I read on eagerly, curious about the sort of person who would waste their time on compiling a list of words you shouldn't ever use (although only seven? Come on, do some work, man!).

Here's their list:

Must, Mustn't, Should, Have, Don't, Can't, Need

What's wrong with them?

They make excuses out of your reasons and dust out of your dreams.

They are mainly expressions of obligation or duty, two concepts that stimulate a severe reaction in the New Agers. Do what you want, not what you must, is their mantra. Be yourself – i.e. whatever you feel like being. I'm not a fan of any 'must do' or 'must have' list and there have been many occasions in my life when I really didn't want to be in a particular place or doing a particular thing, but I absolutely had to, because not being there and not doing those things would have caused far more discomfort and unhappiness. Even if I do end up fulfilling my obligation with bad grace and a sour expression, it's better for the general wellbeing. So

---

*I'm paraphrasing.

135

never wanting to be thought of as a 'happy bunny' by anyone, I will go on using 'don't' and 'can't' (I've based a couple of books on both words already) and most of the others in the list even more frequently, and will look forward to my emotional myxomatosis.

That's How I Roll

'That's how I roll' embodies all the infuriating screw-you attitude of 'whatever' but with a bit more effort required on the part of the Arse from whom it emanates. It involves said Arse having to explain his particular characteristic or trademark behaviour before adding 'that's how I roll'.

'You might not like it … but take it or leave it, that's me … that's how I roll.'

Obviously any normal person would just leave it. I can't imagine a single instance of being won over by an individual's unusual or extreme behaviour just because they explained it with 'that's how I roll'. I think I would even struggle with Jesus if he justified his controversial policy of letting prodigal sons off the hook by adding, 'I tell you most solemnly, that's how I roll.'

Again, because the phrase cloaks the speaker in rakishness and rebellion, many quite ordinary and intelligent people (e.g. geeks) use 'that's how I roll' to scruffy up or harden their image.

Of course, where there are nerds and geeks, there are T-shirts with sarcastic slogans and, whatever your own particularly annoying habit or attribute, there's a 'that's how I roll' T-shirt to make you feel better about it. One which I'm sure is a big hit with certain Americans is 'Shooting deers, drinking beers – that's how I roll'. I would never point out to them that the plural of deer is deer, as having a spelling mistake on your T-shirt is the linguistic equivalent of leaving a mattress in your front garden and just daring someone to stare at it.

One of the very worst of these T-shirts says 'Irish – This is how I roll', with a picture of a paralytic leprechaun surrounded by empty bottles. I don't know how my admirably sober, indigenous Irish relatives feel about that but it's a pretty good representation of expatriate Irish culture and only reinforces my desire to steer clear of them, especially on St Patrick's Day.

As the back pages of the old *NME* taught me, with its ads for T-shirts sporting slogans such as: 'I like the pope, the pope smokes dope', 'Makin' Bacon' (two pigs shagging), 'Shit Happens' and a two-fingered gesture over the word 'Cobblers!', the rule of thumb with any sentence or phrase is: if you can see it on a T-shirt, don't ever say it out loud. *Ever.*

59

Just Be

● ●

This is the sort of phrase which that dreadful, selfish woman probably repeats over and over again somewhere in that terrible book *Eat Pray Love*. 'Just be who you want to be and be true to yourself.' No, I think not, madam. That's what I'd call a recipe for disaster; not so much for an individual but for the whole of society. We can't have people just being who they want – they have responsibilities, for God's sake. Imagine if everyone did that? It's hardly behaviour you'd recommend be enshrined as a Universal Law; Kant would spin so fast in his grave he'd probably drill his way out of it.

People change their mind about who they'd like to be or the situation they'd like to be in about 50 times a day. I frequently think I should jack everything in and be a toymaker in a wooden hut in the Black Forest. At other times, I think I'd like to be Jason Bourne or a gentleman jewel thief or own a hardware shop. I'm sure everyone else is the same. So how do you know that the self you have settled upon as your own, special self is the right one; the one you should 'just be' and to which you should be true (whatever that means)?

I stumbled across this person via her website Just Be Splendid, and I realised she, along with, I am sure, many millions of people like her, had certainly decided she was a particular type of person, albeit one with a terrible grasp of the caps lock function on her keyboard:

This is Me ... liviNg in a DreaM Land full of wishes and hopes ... sLeep in clouds with fairies and ... pLay everyday with colourfuL ballooNs and indulge Myself with cHoco & CottonCandy.

Now, to be fair, it appears as if she enjoys herself a fair bit, but I'd say probably anybody would if they just decided to cut themselves a massive slice of cake and lounge about all day. But that's not going to get the baby bathed or the washing up done, is it, love? Living in a dream world is basically what kids do 90 per cent of the time, because they have no responsibilities and that's what they should be doing. But it's too late for that as adults. My advice to anyone who uses this awful phrase: Don't 'just be', just grow up.

60

Close of Play

● ●

'Close of Play' is, thankfully, a recent alternative to 'at the end of the day' (a phrase so overused throughout the nation that you'd think it had been enforced by law), and, after all the baseball-based metaphors of previous words in the book, at least 'close of play' is an expression from an English game – unless you are one of those people who believe that cricket was invented by Belgians.*

However, I can't help but hear the voice of a public schoolboy whenever I see it written down, and, when spoken, I imagine the voice belonging to a child with a quartered cap, shorts and a blazer. 'Close of play' is when we draw stumps, of course, and head off back to the pavilion where cook has laid on some lemonade and sandwiches.

The working person's dander is raised at the merest mention of 'close of play' because it conveys the idea that what we are doing all day at work is a lark, great fun, a hoot. But more often than not the phrase is used by senior management in the most tedious or unpleasantly stressful of work situations. The email that bounds into a person's inbox on a Friday afternoon requesting the latest

---

*Entirely possible.

distribution figures by 'close of play' is enough to make anyone want to wield a cricket bat in their boss's general direction.

I've been lucky enough to work in advertising, radio and television, where no one does any actual work. Occasionally, there is a panic on – a script is bound with a white plastic spine instead of a black one, or somebody hasn't got the right type of coffee, and then, boy, is the pressure intense! But even in those situations, the utterance of 'I need it by close of play' wouldn't go down too badly as most people working in advertising, radio and television are from public school anyway. But can you imagine, for example, the hard-pressed workers in the call-centre complaints department of BT Broadband – with their thousands of irate calls every minute of the day about the slowness of their connection (often from the same person who, perhaps, requires the internet to research their book)? The employees there would take great exception to their working day being referred to as 'play' when it was anything but.

Is there any acceptable alternative? A word or phrase which means 'when work stops' or 'you can all go home now'? I am quite partial to Malcolm Tucker from *The Thick of It*'s parting shot: 'Off you fuck!' but I think that might cause offence to some people and doesn't quite fit in with the sentence 'I need this by … off you fuck'. Perhaps terminology from some kind of game is the only way forward, but not a posh game like cricket. How about bingo? 'Housey! Housey!' is quite an appropriate call for the time of day we all head for home and bingo is a tad more egalitarian than cricket. So 'Housey!' is on the right lines, but I think we should turn to an even more blue-collar pastime for the solution. Darts. As Martin Amis once wrote, 'Everything I know I have learnt from darts,' and what better way to signal the end of the working day than with the cry 'gaaaaaaame shottttt!'

Girl Crush

Generally these days, the phrase 'girl crush' is used by very strait-laced, control-freaky women in an attempt to make themselves appear edgy without having to put in the hard work (the drinking, the lack of self-control, the low self-esteem). The crush in question is usually on an intelligent, attractive woman who doesn't conform to the conventionally attractive stereotype (Caitlin Moran/Lauren Laverne/Victoria Coren) but the fact is, the woman using the phrase 'girl crush' knows that it makes *her* seem a bit more interesting and 'experimental' to men.

Long after the Lipstick Lesbians, Beth Jordache and Margaret Clemence, had their famous snog in *Brookside* and sent the ratings soaring, publicity-hungry starlets are still ready to suggest a Sapphic side to their sexuality at the drop of a pipe. Lindsay Lohan claimed to be munching the rug for a while and Mrs

Russell Brand (a more precarious job than Chelsea manager) Katy Perry originally shot to fame by bleating 'I Kissed a Girl and I Liked It'

It used to be that any vaguely attractive woman who featured in *Loaded* magazine, from Felicity Kendall to Maria Whittaker, had to spice up the interview by claiming she found it 'very difficult to meet men' and was 'seriously looking for the right guy'. Nowadays, all she has to do is name another famous attractive woman and say she has a 'girl crush' on her and the mucky minds of the *Nuts* readers do the rest.

Girls have always had crushes on their friends – where would *Malory Towers* and *What Katy Did* be without them? But the 'girl crush' of modern usage has little to do with carrying each other's books to prep and punching each other heartily on the shoulder.

There is now a brand of girly products aimed at ten-year-olds called Girl Crush, which includes stuff like airbrush tattoo kits, hair braiders, hair streaking kits and sets of lurid false nails. They are packaged with images of two or three girls together helping each other to tart up and I'm afraid it looks like a man has styled the photoshoot, if you get my meaning.

I'm sure the company behind Girl Crush have no intention other than to help pre-pubescent girls celebrate their friendship but I discovered the Girl Crush range of stuff when I put the phrase into Google and it threw up quite a few images which the manufacturers probably wouldn't want to be associated with.

Like

So much has been written about the infuriatingly indiscriminate use of this word that it's pointless to add to the forest of opinions in print and online. I can overlook the use of 'like' for a pause (it's no worse than 'you know' or 'erm') and the 'like' for emphasis: 'it was like – really cold' (as long as the sentence doesn't end in an upward lilt). But truly unforgivable is:

'I'm like: "yeah" and he was like: "whatever".'

I pray that the word 'like' in this instance is only ever spoken and never actually written down when kids text or email one other. No one could blame the education system for that. Kids are encouraged from a fairly young age to use a variety of ways to attribute speech in storytelling – this is state primary level I'm talking about, not university – not just 'he said, she said'. Apparently there are about 400 different words you can use as an alternative to 'said', but this current generation of ignoramuses has chosen to use a single word – and one that isn't even a verb.

How did this happen? Is it because the young person's visual sense has been overdeveloped to such an extent, having been bombarded since birth with intensely colourful and complex TV and computer images, that they can only reproduce dialogue by re-enacting the scene in front of their audience? When they say, 'I was like: yeah, and she was like: no way,' are they actually saying: 'I was standing like this and speaking and what I said was something like this: yeah'?

Perhaps this pattern of speech is related to the one favoured by a much older generation of predominantly cockney people, which involves a considerable amount of turning around. 'I turned round to him and I said: do what, mate? And he turned round to me and said: gertcha.' I wonder if many years ago ye streetes of olde Londonne townye were once full of cheerful costermongers pirouetting as they exchanged their cheeky banter.

Whatever the possible origins of using 'like' instead of 'said', the real danger is that, coupled with its many other uses, the word 'like' may come to replace dozens of other words until the vocabulary of everyone under 30 dwindles to a dozen or so noises that can only be understood from the tone of voice in which they are said, or should I say 'liked'?

For a terrifying glimpse into this future, cast your mind back to the wonderful but still quite creepy Oliver Postgate puppet show *The Clangers*, in which most of the characters communicated in a swanee whistle. On reflection, I'd still rather have a conversation with a stuffed pink sock than any of today's generation of 'like'-minded people.

63

Do the Math

●●

What is really hateful about this phrase is *not* the assumption that everyone should be able to work things out for themselves (why are people who are good at maths such superior people? 'Come on, it's easy!'), it's the adaptation of the Americanism 'math'. Many linguists would argue that 'math' is just how the Americans say the word and if we are adopting their phrase – just as we would from French or Latin – we should respect that. They would insist that it's no different from *'je ne sais quoi'* and that no one would balk at using that phrase. Well, excuse me, I would. I have no time for those needlessly elaborate foreign phrases that are dropped in conversations as if it was perfectly acceptable to do so – *laissez faire, fin de siècle, primus inter pares* and *sine qua non*. Latin particularly is valued for improving your English vocabulary, so what's the point of padding your English out with untranslated Latin words?

Anyway, yes, I know that 'math' is how the Americans say it; they say a lot of funny words but my point, which I've possibly laboured in this book, is that Americanisms are acceptable out of American mouths (even though millions of Americans hate them too). We on this side of the Atlantic should be happy for them to have their own cultural idiosyncrasies and traditions, which have grown up over hundreds of years, independent of the English and our sense of superiority. But it's also a cultural idiosyncrasy of the English to know that the Americans are always wrong. Mathematics is a plural – so therefore the shortened version should also be plural. 'Steam engines' would not be shortened to 'engine', would it?

You Rock

●●●

There is some confusion about the origin of this term. There are those who think it attributes the rocklike qualities of stability, consistency and reliability which secured the first pope job for St Peter. On this interpretation, 'you rock' is almost interchangeable with 'you star', which is thankfully waning in popularity. However, it's clear to me that 'you rock' means 'you are cool and probably play a musical instrument in a charismatic, rebellious fashion'.

So it's ironic that people who are told that they 'rock' usually do things that decidedly do not rock. People like me. Believe it or not, I have been told that I 'rock' on a number of occasions, mostly by my TV production manager, Julie, who knows full well that, for example, replying to a viewer's letter of complaint or approving an edit schedule is not the behaviour of someone who 'rocks' and she is only saying it to take the piss or make me feel better about myself. Well, I'm sorry, the only people who 'rock' are in rock bands. Wilko Johnson rocks, as does Angus Young out of AC/DC, Chas out of Chas & Dave and the drummer from the Arctic Monkeys.

Don't We, Girls?

There are many, *many* reasons for loathing the daytime ITV show *Loose Women* but the principal one is the audience of hooting harpies to whom the panel of regulars play up shamelessly with coarse double entendres and tawdry observations, always followed by the catchphrase 'Don't we, girls?' It is used to suggest that all the women collectively agree on the same thing, that they're all in cahoots. We all see the joke. 'We like a big one, don't we, girls?' *Loose Women* is like an Ann Summers party attended by the Maenads (literally translated as Ravers) who followed Bacchus around shrieking through the countryside and occasionally tearing men to pieces. We like a bit of orgiastic revelry, don't we, girls?

Some women have a problem with the term 'girl' when applied to anyone over the age of 25. Not as much as I do. 'The girls', 'girly night in' and 'girly weekend' are easily as great an incentive to self-immolate as 'lads' night out'. It might be terribly patronising for me to speak on behalf of the entire opposite sex but I think these terms are a great affront to womankind. For a start, no one who is actually a girl goes on a girly anything. They are definitely all grown women who enjoy 'girly nights in' but they appear to embrace the idea of dressing in the fluffy pink nightwear of a child, eating crap, watching shit on television and drinking decidedly unhealthy drinks. Here is a guide, taken from online, to a 'perfect' girly night in:

1. Ask your girlfriends to bring their PJs, their favourite chick-flick and their best ever dessert or snack. The more fattening and diet-breaking the dessert or snack, the better.
2. Stuffed furry friends are a must.
3. Consider some girly drinks. Baileys is often a girly favourite; on the night, go for it.
4. Regress. It's fun.

If I had written that as a parody, I would have been accused of all sorts of dreadful things from sexism to misogyny to not having a clue about what women are really like. But this is a genuine and fair representation of the thousands of pieces in magazines, weekend supplements and websites devoted to the lobotomising of women, and the phrase 'Don't we, girls?' serves to reflect this even more. It's not attractive, ladies, really it isn't.

Must-Have

● ●

I'm sure this modern phrase, or something like it, has been widely used in the fashion industry for many decades by many a terrifying Gloria Swanson-esque figure in a turban with a cigarette holder swooning, 'Oh, dahling, it's sooo beautiful, you absolutely *must* have it.'

Of course, there is nothing that you 'must have', unless you are a cultural zombie whose every movement, every thought, every whim is controlled by the witch doctor, Fashion; in which case the number of shoes, bags, belts, snoods, shrugs, fabrics and colours you 'must have' is almost infinite. 'This season's must-have citrus brights', 'this autumn's must-have sludgy hues', 'this Michaelmas's must-have jacketeen'. The list could go on.

The fashion editors of national newspapers and magazines act like dealers to the fad addicts. Look at this from the *Daily Mail*:

Want the must-have fashions for next season? Then start shopping now!

If you ever came to understand the time-bending, logical complexities at work in that sentence, your head would explode.

A much simpler proposition to grasp is that not everything

can be 'must-have'; some stuff must be just crap, otherwise the term becomes meaningless. But the tragedy for the fashion journos is that they have very few words to describe so many 'essential' items. Essential itself just isn't urgent enough for them and, apart from 'must-have', what else is there? Sometimes they try 'It's all about' as in 'It's all about the maxi skirt this summer' (what is *it?*) and occasionally they revive the 1950s horror movie poster: 'You thought it had gone away but it's back! [*drum roll please*] The evening jumpsuit!' You can see why they don't use that one very often. So 'must-have' is the 'must-have' expression. The more it occurs, the more desperate and eventually meaningless it becomes, like the word 'legend' or 'genius' or 'awesome' or 'fuck' – it no longer has any power.

In an attempt to rejuvenate their vocabulary, one fashion journalist recently injected some monkey glands into 'must-have' and removed the bandages to reveal something quite repulsive: 'lust-have'. The very typing of this makes me feel so nauseous I can't continue and must have a lie-down.

67

Chick Lit

● ●

'Chick lit' arrived with *Bridget Jones's Diary* in the late 90s, although true fans of the genre will throw their hands up in horror, claiming it was in fact invented two centuries ago by Jane Austen, with her vulnerable but resourceful heroines who can stand on their own two feet. Not sure whether the shoes/chardonnay/shagging elements are all there in Jane Austen, but I wouldn't know as I haven't read any.

I read *Bridget Jones* as a newspaper column, as did several other men I knew, and it was very funny. I had no idea it was a new genre of literature and even when it appeared as a book, and every woman in her late twenties claimed to *be* Bridget Jones, it seemed unnecessary to define it as a genre. Surely men and women bought the same books? Apart from, of course, those blokes who like the shiny-lettered engraved novels as thick as bricks with lots of explosions and the women who read those stories about battered immigrants and kite-flying in Afghanistan.

As soon as the term 'chick lit' appeared and the template of the ideal front cover was collectively agreed upon, dozens of budding authors knew what they were going to write about – a handsome man and a cancelled wedding; would her best mates help the jilted bride or laugh as she falls flat on her face with her Jimmy Blahniks waving in the air?

'Chick lit' is like teen vampire fiction; once it's identified and codified everyone piles in and publishers love it. And, like reality or makeover television programmes, there needs to be just one big hit and then they're off! The need to create a new genre overrides the quality of the individual programming. Often TV commissioners express the desire for something 'genre-busting', but only so they can have a new genre to wave at creative people and say, 'We have a new mould now, squirt your plastic in here!'

Of course, many claim the phrase 'chick lit' was coined on an American university campus as an ironic title for a course in post-feminist literature and as a nod to the 'chick-flick'. And therein lies the whole problem. 'Chick lit' invites you to think that it's a modern ironic take on those romantic happy-ever-after stories for girls. The self-deprecating 'chick' understands that the gaudy covers with the jaunty typeface disguise stories featuring heroines with real heart who can occasionally say something meaningful about what it's like to be a modern woman. Stories like *Shoedunnit?*, *Mr Right Now-ish*, *Delete at the End of the Tunnel* and *If He's Rich Enough I'll Shag Him.**

There's usually a girl who gets a bit pissed with her mates and, tottering around at a posh art exhibition, bumps into a tousle-haired attractive art historian. So as not to appear a fool she blags her way through the evening and then a series of dates with absolutely no knowledge of Art (obviously we wouldn't believe that she'd know anything) and, in a slightly kooky but lovable way, she teaches him a lesson about beauty being in the eye of the beholder. So it's definitely not Mills and Boon. Except that it is.

---

*All made up, but for a few quid I'll have a go at one.

Big Beast

A couple of months ago, I remember passing a huge estate agent's sign on an ostentatious plate-glass office block in Mayfair that read: 'Room for the big beasts to move around'. Clearly designed to appeal to anyone arrogant or twattish enough in the business or banking world (I know that doesn't narrow it down much) to think they deserved the massive office and the title 'big beast'. But if ever the majesty and dignity of a lion or a silverback gorilla or a bull elephant could be diminished it is by the application of this phrase to politicians or bankers. And who originally applied it? Despite the fact that it has been used by numerous journalists, it almost certainly was put about by a politician in the first place. Someone who probably fancied himself as a 'big beast' and regarded his rivals as pygmy shrews or bush babies. Big beasts are as mythical as the Tory Grandees who are occasionally called upon to slit the gizzard of a weakening leader. These are the top toffs in the party who are supposed to have done for Thatcher and Iain Duncan Smith, but the title is exposed as a tawdry piece of self-promotion when you realise that these people are the likes of Malcolm Rifkind, John Wakeham and Chris Patten. If Tory Grandees exist at all nowadays, they are the nincompoops with

RICHARD WILSON

moats and duck houses bought with dodgy expenses claims.

When I hear the phrase 'big beast', I'm reminded of the great scene in *Airplane 2* when William Shatner's character is reflecting on the hero Striker and calls him 'the big man, el numero uno honcho, the head cheese'. These are all titles that have been awarded by total arseholes to themselves without any irony over the last 50 years. But who exactly is a 'big beast'? If you Google the term and have the parental controls on your search engine, you will only get one result: Ken Clarke. Likeable though he is for his cigars, brown suede shoes and indifference to putting his foot in it, there is only one reason to call Ken Clarke a big beast and that is his big belly. Oh, and his big face and his big arse. Believe it or not, the hilariously named Ed Balls is now being touted as a big beast – probably by himself through some judicious press briefings – simply because he has verbally roughed up a few people and is a bit of a bully. There is nothing majestic about Ed Balls and the only animal I can compare him to has eponymously piggy eyes. Like Ken Clarke, he is, as Richard Ingrams wrote in a smart definition of 'big beast', 'a failed politician with a grudge'.

Alpha Male

Zoologists define the 'alpha male' as the top of the hierarchy in a community of social animals such as wolves or apes. He is the first to eat and the first, sometimes the only one, allowed to mate. The beta males defer to the alphas and, in some species, actually help them mate without getting the chance to do so themselves.

What a surprise, then, that the concept of the 'alpha male', which you might occasionally hear in a business or political context, is most frequently discussed on websites offering shitty dating advice to desperate blokes. Whatever the social, behavioural and genetic complexities in the animal kingdom, in the world of dating, 'alpha male' = success with women, 'beta male' = loser with sand kicked in your face and everyone laughing and pointing at you.

In the 60s and 70s, the solution to this condition was still the Charles Atlas Body Building Course – an hour a day's 'dynamic tension' and plenty of enemas – but now it's the websites with names like Mandatetip.com and Easykopoff.org who are coming to the rescue of the single man. A bit like the Charles Atlas ads with the 97lb weakling, they tell you that: 'You don't want to be a beta male – otherwise known as an average guy.

Attractive women don't go for average guys.' Of course, women are attracted to money, fame, power and looks, but a website can't help you pick those up very easily so they tell you that 'success with women is all in the mind'. Which makes it so much easier to peddle bullshit.

In an online advice column called 'Get the Habits of Alpha Males', we are told that 'alpha males' 1) talk slow, 2) stick their chin out, and 3) ask a lot of questions. Sounds very like a stupid person to me and a bit of a Neanderthal. But of course what they really mean is an inquisitive, confident, firm-jawed fellow, rather than a great big dork. 'Alpha males' show leadership; they are in control of situations and, above all, put women at their ease.

All those attributes may indeed be attractive to women, but to classify them as peculiar to 'alpha males' in the zoological sense is nonsense. It's like saying women are attracted to attractive men. 'Alpha male' is just a label given a laminated sheen with a bit of cod-science.

We can all blame zoologist Desmond Morris for this with his bloody Apewatching/Manwatching/We're All Just Gibbons under the skin/Human Zoo twaddle. The attractiveness to the females of an 'alpha male' ape is superior strength and intelligence; the ability to grab something to eat that the others can't and rip the arms and legs off any would-be challenger. It's got nothing to do with imposing yourself on a room, staring out of the window while others are talking, placing your hands on your hips, and noticing a woman has had her hair done. Interestingly, one dating advice website may have begun to acknowledge this based on the evidence of this entry:

The guys who join math teams or play chess at lunch are usually the beta males and may be thought less attractive by girls. But it should be noted that 'nerds' are becoming increasingly popular. As long-term mates or 'boyfriends', they stereotypically on average tend to be nicer and more respectful toward girls.

Ha! Go figure.

70

Intern

• •

This is someone who works in a big office for free, offering help and assistance to senior people while getting interesting on-the-job experience. Monica Lewinsky perhaps is the most famous 'intern' and I suppose that's a fair description of what she did.

Of course, it's another American word which we have no business using. As someone who grew up in the early 1970s, I thought an 'intern' was a Northern Irish Catholic who was locked up without trial.

The correct word is, of course, trainee, but that probably doesn't sound swanky enough for those companies who prefer to disguise the fact that they are squeezing ten hours a day out of an ambitious but probably penniless graduate for nothing. Also 'trainee' suggests that they might actually be trained to do something useful, whereas most office jobs nowadays, no matter whether they are in law, banking, accountancy, insurance or the media, involve sitting at a computer and playing Angry Birds on an iPhone when the boss isn't looking.

Carbs

●●●

I will just about accept 'carbs' from mechanics as in 'twin carbs' (meaning two carburettors), but as a shortened form of carbohydrate this is just not on. It's as if the 'hydrate' part of the word is so insignificant as to allow it to be jettisoned like the polystyrene punnet of a jacket potato. Without the hydrate, we'd just be eating carbon.

Fitness instructors, personal trainers and sports coaches will discuss the importance of 'carbs' as readily as they do with 'pecs', 'glutes' and 'abs' (see p. 121). 'Get some carbs on board, you've got a tough day ahead,' you'll hear them say, or 'You're bulky for your height, you're going to have to cut down on the carbs.' Yes, and oh don't forget while you're at it, you'll need the right balance of protes and, er, fatsies. And the mins and the vits too.

Why do usually sane and well-educated people feel the need to be on such horribly matey terms with dietary essentials; it's as if Jamie Oliver had been reincarnated as a science teacher and invented a whole new way of speaking: 'Wazz in a few carbs and get their old enzyme mucker amylase to break 'em down into yer glucose and yer sucrose.'

I tried to find a useful web discussion for the acceptability of the abbreviation of 'carbs' but at every single mention of the word hundreds of nutters obsessed about their weight came piling in and the real issue – the atrophy of the English language – got pushed aside.

Risk-Averse

● ●

Another term from the financial world that more and more people are using in an attempt to make their life sound exciting enough for Robert Peston to do a report on it: 'Mrs Thomas from Marchmont Street revealed today that, when it comes to letting her 12-year-old son walk the 100 yards to school, she is quite risk-averse.'

'Risk-averse' implies that Mrs Thomas has weighed up all the pros and cons, studied the FTSE index for the last ten years, taken the temperature of the global economy and checked the value of sterling against the zloty and decided, nah, I'll take him in the car.

I completely understand Mrs Thomas's reluctance to let her child walk to school, but what is wrong with the word 'cautious'? Is it not macho enough? Is the pseudo-scientific mumbo-jumbo spouted by the City's Masters of the Universe more attractive? For example:

'I'm not having a chicken madras because, when it comes to the spiciness of dishes from the subcontinent, I'm quite risk-averse.'
'Taking into account the high incidence of minor accidents following more than two pints of bitter, I'll forego the one last half because I'm quite risk-averse.'
'I know that Lidl is much closer to our house than the Waitrose, but, when it comes to balancing the cost savings on chicken drumsticks against appearing to be a pikey, I'm quite risk-averse.'

Or do people think 'cautious' just makes them sound like a scaredy cat? I love the word cautious and I'm proud to be it. Caution is the single most important virtue in modern life. Taking risks pays dividends for a small minority but the majority always suffer. There are numerous proverbs and sayings – and Guinness ads – that testify to the truth: that every situation improves for everyone involved if they all just wait for a bit.

Yummy Mummy

●●●●●●●●●●●●●●●●●●●●●●●●●●●●●●●●●●●●●●●

This is almost certainly a term coined by the people it describes. No woman, nay mother, would call themselves a MILF ... but who would object to being called a 'yummy mummy'? Apart from someone with no kids, perhaps. Or a man.

From the rhyming dictionary of some unknown postpartum journo (although someone will no doubt claim it), the concept of the 'yummy mummy' has turned into a huge job-creation scheme for stay-at-home, part-time journalist mums, some of whom can write about how hard it is to stay a 'yummy mummy', juggling kids, house, 'me time' and husband (who pays for it all), while others can write about how they are really quite slovenly and *not at all* like other 'yummy mummies', as they belong to a completely different marketing sub-branch of 'slummy mummies'.

'Yummy mummy' is one of those handy labels like 'yuppie' that doesn't really fit anyone properly. There are no particular attributes we can tick off. People may think they know one when they see one but you could never hold up a yuppie to close examination and find that he ticked all the boxes. I'm saying this partly because in the late 80s I was walking along a street in central London wearing a suit and horn-rimmed spectacles. Some rugby league fans from Wigan happened to be in town that day because it was the eve of the Cup Final and when they saw me they all pointed, shouting, 'Look, a fookin' Yoopy.' I was young, possibly even urban, but certainly not upwardly mobile. Remember the red braces-wearing city worker who always appears in those TV archive shows which mention the 80s (cue Pet Shop Boys 'Let's Make Lots of Money'). He was probably the only one to wear those braces at the time but we all think the whole of London dressed like that. The label fits the idea of a person we'd like to have nicely categorised for us, so that we can dislike them more easily. And sell them stuff.

If proof were needed about the umbilical connection between 'yummy mummy' and marketing, it's the website Yummymummy.org, the logo of which is three cupcakes. Bloody cupcakes! They are everywhere! Gift shops, coffee shops, who have just come back from holiday in America, anywhere that 30-plus women might frequent, are all heaving with cupcakes these days. Nigella is partly responsible (see 'Goddess' p. 89). This famously fanciable mum with baking skills chose the cupcake (fnaar!) as the design motif for her breakthrough book *The Domestic Goddess*. If ever there was a visual metaphor for the mouth-watering mother figure, it's the pert pink cupcake with a cherry topping. Which is weird, as mothers have been baking stuff for centuries without arousing men to the point of them needing to have to knock one out.

Rocking That Look/ Working That Look

● ●

As explained in 'You Rock' (see p. 147), the word 'rock' in these phrases has no real connection with rock in the AC/DC sense of the word, however much it tries. 'Rocking that look' can be achieved by any woman wearing a leather jacket and/or jeans. And sometimes not even that. Flicking through my pile of women's mags, I read this paragraph beneath a picture of a woman in what

I would probably call a skirt, a blouse and some sunglasses:

How to rock the look: this new look is cool in a Kim Wilde-tomboy-meets-
Debbie Harry-mature-femme way.

When I read this, my first question was: do they mean that Kim Wilde who used to do the Channel 5 gardening programme? And my second question was: *mature femme* – is that a hygiene product? My third question was: does 'rocking a look' mean just wearing any old collection of clothes, regardless of their association with motorbikes, guitars and leather jackets, as long as the model looks a bit petulant? The next piece in the 'How to Rock the Look' article supplied the answer:

Complete the look with Jeggings – stretch denim in a legging cut, with a
higher waistband than jeans. The waistband is elasticated …

Leggings with an elasticated waistband? Yes, because a rock chick never knows when she might find herself feeling a bit bloated backstage at the 100 Club.

So, with a few carefully chosen stylish but comfortable items, you can join the ranks of the great rock'n'roll stars of legend. No biting off of bats' heads is required, no stomping around a model of Stonehenge or firing the neck of your guitar into the audience like an RPG; 'rocking that look' is as facile a way to talk up the clothes a person is wearing as 'working that look'.

'Gwen Stefani has been working that look for years,' claimed an idiot fashion reporter on a celebrity mag I read recently. Yes, what had happened was poor Gwen was slaving away in a combination of some sort of floaty, tie-dye top with some kind of complementary trousers and another columnist claimed she was copying the style of some other celebrity (Lori Petty?). The fashion reporter was nobly springing to Gwen's defence. And quite right too. Poor Gwen – all that hard graft she put in by, er … wearing some clothes and some other bitch tries to take the credit. It seems, in the world of the celebrity/fashion journalist, that 'working that look' just means 'wearing the same clothes all the time'. I have, by that token, been working the dark-blue/black/grey shapeless stuff from Next Directory for about fifteen years.

Comfort Zone

What I really hate about 'comfort zone' is not the phrase so much as the thinking behind its creation. I try not to use the word 'zone' if at all possible unless I'm referring to the demilitarised area of Korea in the 1950s, the area covered by my resident's parking permit, or the sector of the London Underground map I'm travelling to or from. The problem with 'zone' is that you are one step away from discussing whether or not you are 'in the zone' – a meaningless piece of bollocks from not you are 'in the zone' – a meaningless piece of bollocks from sports psychology. 'Comfort zone' is also much favoured by shrinks and motivational coaches from all walks of life – sport, business, education, politics or the media.

The only point of the 'comfort zone' for these people is to take other people out of it. For some reason, continuing to do something or be somewhere that we enjoy and find relaxing is a bad thing. Here is a diagram drawn by a motivational coach who preaches his mind-healing nonsense on the internet:

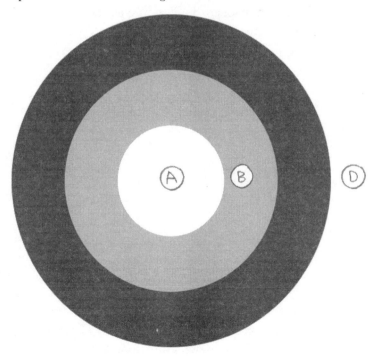

A = Comfort Zone, B = Uncomfortable Zone,
D = Danger Zone!

Obviously, the big Area A in the picture is the comfort zone. And what do we associate with 'comfort'? Good things like ease, stability, security and relaxation. Brilliant. But no – the motivational coach asks us, 'Does it not also mean sameness, boredom and stagnation?' Er, no. It means comfort; which is what normal people aspire to all their lives. The motivational coach really wants to take you into Area B where, he admits, there is stress, anxiety and fear. But that's great too, because 'that's where change happens, that's where you learn things'. Yes, a change has happened – I've experienced fear, anxiety and stress and I don't like it now. The only lesson I've learned is, I'm not leaving my 'comfort zone' again – or Area A as I prefer to call it.

The unlabelled Area C must be worse than stress/anxiety/fear but not as bad as danger. It's probably 'embarrassment' and I don't think even a motivational coach could argue there are positives to be drawn from that.

Area D is designated as the 'danger zone', so God knows what that involves. Suicide bombing? That would certainly be uncomfortable and a bit of a challenge for most people. Who knows what we could learn? That Osama Bin Laden was right and there are 72 virgins waiting in paradise?

Take-out/To Go

● ●

'Let's get a take-out.'

No, I'm not eating that.

A take-away is fine but I'm not eating a 'take-out'. I'm not going on a date with it; we're not going to the cinema or bowling. I'm taking it away to eat somewhere else.

'Is that to go?'

No, *I'm* going to go when you've put it in the bag. I'm going to go out of the kebab shop and eat it at the bus stop and possibly spill mint yoghurt down me.

I'm particularly irritated by 'to go' as nobody in Britain ever goes up to the counter and asks for any kind of dish or drink and adds 'to go'. The very idea is ridiculous: 'Two cod, three chips, a saveloy, mushy peas and some scraps to go please, cock.'

No, the use of 'to go' has been foisted upon the poor sales staff, who in turn parrot it at the customer, by the evil corporate food chains; the sort of companies that take over the catering of large institutions like the BBC or British Rail or the NHS and force their staff to wear embarrassing uniforms and say things like 'have a nice day' and 'enjoy your meal'. I was working at BBC Radio when the catering was contracted out to some dreadful firm called Synthopak or something, who gleefully embraced such customer-service twaddle, and the look on the faces of us grizzled staff as we were told to 'enjoy your meal' and asked if our 14p cup of weak tea was 'to go' was priceless.

I do fear for the word 'go'. I've counted the number of entries in this book featuring that combination of two innocent letters 'g' and 'o' and I have the feeling it's becoming the most ill-treated word in the English language, suffering more public humiliation and abuse than Karl Pilkington. I think I shall start a campaign for the prevention of cruelty to 'GO' and donate to it all the royalties I receive from this book.*

*After expenses.

To Die For

● ●

The 1995 Nicole Kidman film of the same name actually had some merit because at least it was about ambition and the fatal lengths to which some people will go to achieve fame. But roast potatoes 'to die for'? Limestone flooring 'to die for'? Of course, it was never meant to be about roast potatoes, it was supposed to be the fashion world's desperate attempt to hype up the shreds of leather, wool and plastic it likes to call 'next season's hot look'. Whenever you hear a ghastly phrase like this, you know you are only a shriek away from the monsters of *Sex in the City*, a TV show that as far as I could see existed purely to boost chlamydia awareness. 'Every single bag, shoe, outfit is to die for.' That's from a young American reality TV star called Khloe Kardashian – and a Paris Hilton-esque space-waster – whom I'd never heard of until I began writing this book. *Sex in the City* is her favourite TV show and this is not the only thing that makes her a very irritating person indeed. It turns out that she uses almost every phrase in this book about ten times a day. I would urge you to go and check her out purely for a laugh but I don't want to be seen to be encouraging her.

Forget handbags and potatoes and anything Ms Kardashian ever says, 'to die for' should only ever be reserved for freedom, faith and family.

78

I'm Loving It

● ●

I spoke to respected linguist Professor David Crystal about this phenomenon and he, I'm sad to say, is loving the fact that more and more people are 'loving it'. He says they have found a way of expanding the language without expanding the vocabulary. By clever use of present continuous tense, they have extended their love and strengthened it, because they are continuing to love something in a way that 'love' just doesn't convey. An elegant explanation but I'm pretty sure it would be lost on the average 'loving it' lover.

What is far less elegant but easier to grasp is that millions of idiots around the world are only familiar with the present continuous tense of the verb 'to love' thanks to one of the most pernicious advertising campaigns in history: McDonald's 'I'm Lovin' It'. You would think that the smug warbling of tiny-headed twat Justin Timberlake combined with that vomit-inducing five-note whistle would have been a major turn-off for any vaguely sentient being, and you'd be right, but we are dealing with people who would go out of their way to eat a cheeseburger for breakfast, lunch and/or dinner. In full knowledge of the effect they were having, McDonald's took one of the most powerful, beautiful, simple words and turned it into a catchphrase for morons.

It's impossible to avoid the phrase now. It's spread throughout teen culture and fully grown adults are passing it around like a joint at a North London dinner party. Sometimes just to rub salt into the wounds of English-lovers, an individual will even throw in an unnecessary 'we', as in 'we're loving that'. They are the sort of people who deserve to remain single for the rest of their lives.

Whenever I hear 'I'm loving it', I can't help but be reminded of Rangi Ram, the politically incorrect Indian bearer from *It Ain't Half Hot Mum* (in real life, Urdu-speaking white Englishman Michael Bates). He was the cheerful narrator of the sitcom who yielded to no one in his admiration of the Imperial British and prided himself on his mastery of their language. In between stupendously phlegmy throat-clearings, Rangi would wobble his head from side to side and say things like, 'I am loving your English weather, Sergeant Major sahib.' Or 'Be sitting up straight, you punka-wallah, and don't be such clever dicky.'

So, if you want to give the impression that English is your second language, be like Rangi and carry on loving it.

79

24/7

● ●

I'm afraid it's too late to stop this one. To paraphrase the German theologian Martin Niemoller: When they began saying 'cool' I did not speak out because no one I knew said 'cool'. When they began saying 'awesome' I did not speak out because no one I knew said 'awesome'. When they began saying '24/7' I did not speak out because no one I knew had ever said it. But then John Humphrys said it on the *Today* programme and I thought – that's it, we're buggered.

Has it arisen out of text-speak or teen language or because in this modern digital age two digits cost more than one? Who knows? It's now rife throughout the entire world.

The Wikipedia entry for '24/7' says that there has been 'criticism of some companies for claiming they are open for business 24/7 when only an automated answer service is available'. No, that's not the main reason for criticism. It's because they are contributing to the spread of this ridiculous way of communicating.

But there is no reason to speak like this – we are not charged a penny a letter to communicate with each other. New York's longitude and latitude is 42 degrees north and 74 degrees west but no one would say 'I'm off to 42/74 for my holidays', although I'm sure Big Brother would tell them it was 'Doubleplusgood thinking'.

The widespread adoption of '24/7' has held the doors open for 'no-brainer', 'end of' and 'let's park that'. Texting language and the spread of hip-hop and DJ culture has accelerated the abbreviation of words and the introduction of numbers into sentences, to the point where we seem to be living in an age where even car registration plates are more eloquent than a lot of human beings.

80

Shout-Out

●●●●●●●●●●●●●●●●●●●●●●●●●●●●●●●●●●●●●●

A 'shout-out' is a stupid idiot's way of saying thank you or acknowledging someone else's presence. It's a phrase which is entirely appropriate for young people to use (with the usual proviso that they don't do so within earshot of me) because it's exactly the sort of thing a seven-year-old kid would do when he sees his mate in the street. He shouts, 'Hey! Sammy! Hey! Sammy!' until Sammy notices and says, 'What?' and then the kid just says hello. The absurdity of the 'shout-out' is admirably demonstrated in the *Alan Partridge* episode when he keeps shouting 'Dan!' at his alter ego Dan, becoming ever more desperate as he fails to be acknowledged.

'Shout-out' probably has its cultural origins in DJ-ing as a replacement for the old-fashioned 'request'. I'm assuming sending a postcard to Peter Powell at Radio 1 is beyond the memory of all but the most grizzled of readers – 'Can I say hello to my friend Sharon and everyone who knows me?' 'You just have!' And perhaps people in their thirties still have vague memories of staggering up to the DJ in a nightclub and asking for 'Ride On Time' or some other popular tune from the hit parade. If the DJ was an obliging sort, he would probably relay the request over the PA, dipping the volume of the incoming track in the traditional cheesy style (a technique shown to its best effect with 'Hi-Ho Silver Lining'). However, in recent years, the sound in clubs has grown louder and louder and the noise more incessant as PAs have been replaced by 'Sound Systems' (I don't really know. I'm making most of this up; I haven't been in a nightclub since 1996). And if the DJ is ever going to talk over the music it will have to be for a really important reason; for example, to give 'a big shout-out to my man Lennox for the doobie', which means 'Thank you, Lennox, my old friend, for providing the excellent refreshments.' Lennox would then be able to acknowledge the cheers of the crowd who would all then be eager to get the DJ to give their mates a 'shout-out' too. Thus, 'giving a big shout' to an individual or a posse has become just a way of publicly recognising that a person is 'in the house'. It's basically just like nodding at someone you pass in the street only much noisier and more irritating.

Just as some words and phrases are acceptable for Americans to use but sound appalling coming from British mouths, so 'shout-out' is just about tolerable from a club DJ but only ever ridiculous when it comes from the kind of white middle-class acting/singing imbecile who gives a 'shout-out' from the podium of an awards do. Barely a week goes by without some dippy starlet giving a 'shout-out' to their stylist or personal trainer, or someone like Christian Bale is giving a 'shout-out' at the Oscars to his boxing coach. Can you imagine Marlon Brando winning the Oscar for *On The Waterfront* and giving 'a shout-out to my man Karl Malden for his great supporting work'?

Unbelievably, in London now there is an awards do called the Shout Out Awards. These aren't for the best/loudest/most irritating shout-out; they are awards for genuinely good works – environmental campaigns, community action, etc., but they call them the Shout Out Awards to give the winners some extra credibility which their good works obviously can't quite deliver. Even worse – last year they were presented by crusty, white, middle-aged newsreader Jon Snow, and with that one example you have the whole raison d'être for this book. Jon Snow announcing, 'Welcome to this year's Shout Out Awards' is as close as you can get to an old man in black tie pogo-ing in a marquee to 'Anarchy in the UK'. I wonder if he whooped as he said it.

The phrase seems to have even less meaning in the community of YouTubers – those annoying middle-class kidults who litter the internet with their useless videos. In their world it appears to mean simply 'mention'. You can find on YouTube something called 'The Greatest Shoutout Video Ever'. In it a teenage girl references other YouTube user names by writing them on Post-its and sticking them all over her bedroom. That's it. She actually posted a request online for people to send her their monickers so she could feature them and thousands did. Just to get mentioned. You would think the generation who have grown up with more sophisticated media and means to access it than the creators of *Star Trek* could scarcely have dreamed of would demand a much higher level of personal satisfaction from their online digital interface experience, but no – just a mention will do, and not even from anyone as famous as Peter Powell.

Go Figure

● ●

See elsewhere on the shocking abuse of the word 'go'. 'Go figure', along with similarly ironically detached phrases like 'you do the math', 'wake up and smell the coffee', 'stop and smell the flowers', 'go take a swim in lake you' and the other popular Americanisms are very often exhortations because Americans are always urging people on. Optimism and enthusiasm are defining characteristics of the American personality. This is often referred to as their 'can-do attitude'. What's more, they all love being told what to do by each other. The normal British response to being told to 'wake up and smell the coffee' is 'piss off', but an American would think – 'yeah, thanks, I'll go do that right now.' It's ironic that in the Land of the Free they are always bossing each other about.

This is a good point to mention 'boosters' and 'knockers'. Yes, madam. Boosters are an American phenomenon from the latter part of the 19th century and some still exist today. They were mainly local businessmen who organised themselves into groups to heavily promote their local town as a place for people to live, do business and prosper. They wore badges with positive slogans, they printed banners, hung up bunting and plastered stickers all over the place; they drove floats and wore boaters with promotional messages. In fact, they probably invented the modern idea of 'promotional merchandise'. The American author Sinclair Lewis wrote in his great 1922 novel *Babbitt* about a Boosters Lunch in the fictional city of Zenith.

As each of the four hundred Boosters entered he took from a wallboard a huge celluloid button announcing his name, his nickname, and his business. There was a fine of ten cents for calling a Fellow Booster by anything but his nickname at a lunch.

In the booster's world the worst thing anyone could be was a knocker; someone who didn't talk up his local town or business colleagues, someone who was cynical and negative and who thought being obliged to call a person by his nickname was a bit stupid and annoying. Sound like anyone you know? Like you, for instance, or almost any other English person? We are knockers and the Americans are boosters. Oliver Hardy is often a booster and Stan is a knocker, albeit accidentally. Stan Laurel, of course, is English. The English have never needed slogans and exhortations like 'Go for it!' and 'Way to go!' because traditionally we've preferred to understate our own achievements and keep our emotions in check. We have also always known that, if we behaved otherwise, everyone else would be saying under their breath, 'What a twat.' Until now. We must not allow boosterism – embodied in phrases like 'you do the math' and 'go figure' – to creep in and erode our character. We should be proud of our knockers.

Cash Rich, Time Poor

● ●

'Time poor' is used abundantly now in middle management by people who are clearly so pressed for time that they are unable to use the two-syllable word 'busy', even though it takes exactly the same amount of effort to say.

My first encounter with it came a few years, and a couple of changes of address ago.* I was doing some building work on my house and my next-door neighbour wasn't happy about it. He and his wife's main concern was, understandably, that they didn't want their Saturday mornings disturbed by noisy building work. It was absolutely right to insist on that but then my neighbour added: 'Our weekends are important to us because we are quite time poor.'

Now, this phrase is bad enough on its own but what made it even worse on this occasion was the bit he left out. 'Time poor' is nearly always preceded by 'cash rich'. He knew it and I knew it. The unspoken words were: 'We are cash rich, time poor. We work so hard earning all our money that when we are at home we don't want our relaxation to be disturbed by you, who obviously have loads of time on your hands and, by the looks of

---

*i.e. the people described are not my current neighbours.

you, can't be earning very much money.'

I've always been puzzled (read annoyed) by people who bellyache about how many hours they work, when they earn shitloads of money. At the heart of their complaint is that they cannot spend the money they earn, so the simple answer is – don't do it then. If time means more to you than money, jack in the highly paid job and do something you like that's easier and allows you to knock off at 5.00 p.m. The fact is, earning wheelbarrows full of cash is why many people go to work in the first place and they make a conscious decision to choose money over leisure time.

I suspected at the time that, if my 'cash-rich' neighbours were suddenly to become 'time rich' as well, they would struggle to know what to do with themselves. Fortunately for them and their ilk, someone invented the Blackberry, the iPhone and online poker so that any fresh spare time/money they might acquire could be squandered with much less effort.

Genius/Legend

It's been said often enough that these are vastly overused terms; as the football pundits say, we're running out of superlatives. Genuine 'geniuses' are exceptionally rare and true 'legends' are born once in a lifetime. However, the usage I particularly object to is of these nouns as adjectives. I have banged on at great length elsewhere about the noun-as-verb problem but this is, if anything, more serious. Increasing numbers of people out there – and they don't all suffer from the handicap of being young – are saying 'he's genius' and 'she's legend'.

The grammatical error with these words is compounded by the aforementioned problem of excessively widespread attribution of 'genius' and 'legend' to the wrong people. The people who are idiotic enough to use the noun as an adjective are also applying it to people who are in no way 'genius' or 'legend'. Usually they are people like someone's mate Chris. 'Oh yes, Chris, he's legend.' How come? He probably walked along a high wall once while completely pissed and then vomited spectacularly somewhere. Some irredeemably annoying people might even suggest that Chris is 'ledge'. And someone else's mate Lucy is 'genius' because she can drink a pint through the material of her T-shirt or get the whole of a half-pint glass in her mouth.

Some linguists argue that it's the same as saying 'that's magic' but the sense of that is, 'if you want to know what proper magic is, look no further'. If people were watching Wayne Rooney in a football match and saying 'that's (i.e. that piece of skill) genius', it wouldn't bother me so much, but they don't; they say 'Rooney's genius'. Whereas the truth is Rooney's arsehole.

Quality Time

●●

This is not quite as bad as 'me time' but it's getting there. In fact, it complements 'me time', which is for the selfish parent lounging in a bath eating chocolate or watching some terrible film in their home cinema; while 'quality time', or 'QT' as it has been horrendously abbreviated to, is what people who use this phrase wish to spend with their kids or their spouse, as opposed to just good old-fashioned Greenwich Mean Time.

I imagine the people who use 'quality time' actually timetable it in their diaries:

> *3 p.m. to 5 p.m. Saturday 17th – quality time with kids.*
> *TO DO: Reminiscences / family catchphrases / spontaneity*

And of course, as any busy executive appreciates, anything in the diary can be rescheduled if necessary, so if the dad hasn't had time to work up any decent family reminiscences he can always say something's come up at work and is it OK to cancel, son?

On a website about fatherhood, there are some surprising tips on how dads can spend 'quality time' with their kids, two of which are 'stay in for the evening' and 'eat together'. Without appearing self-righteous, these seem like fairly basic things that a father should do anyway, which points out even further the absurdity of the phrase: the word 'quality' has no function and just spending 'time' has a lot more meaning.

Space

● ●

I blame Kevin McCloud for this one. Much as I love Channel 4's *Grand Designs* and Kevin's TV manner, he has given a platform for loads of architects and pretentious self-builders to turn the word 'space' into one of the most annoying words in the English language.

As they all sit around at the end of the programme and the

camera shots dissolve into each other as if it were property-porn, a look of utter smugness flits across the faces of the owners ('we were on time and under budget') Hamish and Cathy, as they tell Kevin: 'I think we're really growing into the space.' They move to the garden: 'I really love this,' says Kevin as he slides open a massive glass door with his little finger: 'Yes, it really harmonises the outdoor space with the indoor space.' Kevin goes upstairs into a bedroom the size of a B&Q: 'What a lovely space!' as I'm screaming: 'Room! Room! It's a bloody room!'

For a discipline that is supposed to sit comfortably with progress, the poncy world of architecture and design has changed very little since the early 80s when I was a trainee in an advertising agency. I would often look puzzled in front of a piece of creative work and ask the art director why they'd left a big empty space on one side of the layout for the ad. 'Space? That's a design element. Don't you know anything?'

Architects are forever complaining that ordinary people don't/can't (you choose) appreciate the beauty of their work, but they can hardly be surprised when they talk so much crap about the dynamic of the building, the shape grammar of the structure, the narrative of the materials and the integrity of the 'space'.

I may be wilfully misunderstanding what they mean but to me, 'space', like a lot of the language of architecture, is empty.

Madge

• •

Is 'Madge' a term of endearment or designed to irritate Madonna? There were tabloid reports that she hated it so much that she left the country, although one suspects that's more to do with Guy Ritchie rather than the nickname. While 'Madge' was living and working in Britain, she did Madonna no harm at all. 'Madge' suggested to the *Heat*-obsessed public that she was an ordinary (and honorary) British person who just happened to occasionally nip off to Malawi to buy children in between making eye-gougingly bad films. She absorbed the nickname as part of her whole self-promotional machine.

Some showbiz journalists have suggested she loved it because she thought it was a reference to 'Her Majesty' and even went so far as to wear a tracksuit with the word embroidered on it. I like the idea that Madonna thought 'Madge' might have been cockney rhyming slang for a female body part, which would have been appropriate as, Lord knows, she flashes it often enough.

I don't care whether Madonna likes it or not, I hate it because it was coined in the years of 'The Great Stink' – the early 00s (never say the Noughties) – when the streets were littered with nothing but shitty celebrity stories from publications like

Heat and *OK!* and TV programmes like *Big Brother,* and when it was impossible to avoid the depressing personal lives of Jade Goody, Kerry Katona, Jordan and the Beckhams. These people are still hovering around the periphery of our consciousness today and the effluent from celebrity magazines still contaminates our once beautiful language. Bandying around famous people's nicknames as if they were personal friends does nothing but perpetuate their existence still further.

Just Got

● ●

> *The Best Just Got Better*
> *Garlic Just Got Tastier*
> *Broadband Just Got Faster*
> *Art Just Got Bigger*

Five years ago, you would have been able to say with certainty that these were all taken from American adverts. Now you could just as easily hear this kind of self-conscious hip-pop speak from BBC news journalists and even BBC weathermen. 'The winds just got windier,' says Daniel Corbett. Really? Just a second ago, was it? Did they do it sneakily while we weren't looking?

It's understandable that advertising copy, especially American advertising copy, tries to create a sense of urgency in the consumer so that, whatever it is, they must buy it NOW, but why do we adopt it so readily and inappropriately in this country? I keep wanting to stop the culprits, give them a slap and say, 'Do it again and, remember: it HAS just got better.'

I'm waiting with grim expectancy for the worst example of this phrase to surface in everyday British life. In the Will Smith/Martin Lawrence buddy/cop movie *Bad Boys II*, one of the characters mutters: 'Shit just got real.' There are so many grammatical and cultural problems with this phrase for right-thinking British people that you'd think it could never possibly establish itself. But I know that, one day, someone well educated and likeable will use it without any hint of irony within my earshot. I just hope it's not John Simpson who finishes another doom-laden report about the Middle East descending into chaos again with 'Shit just got real ... this is John Simpson, reporting live from Ras Lanuf, Libya.' Then some idiot can safely say: 'The English language just got dumber.'

88

Park

I first heard this word used in this context from Peter Mandelson when he was Secretary of State for Northern Ireland. We weren't chatting, I should point out. I don't want to give the impression that we're mates.

To avoid missing a deadline for a resolution to power-sharing, Mandelson decided to 'park' the talks between the Catholics and the Protestants rather than have them fail. A shrewd but characteristically tricksy move from one of British politics' smoothest operators and a clever, if deceptive, use of language. Now, however, the same tactic of using 'park' as a verb is in constant use by smooth and devious operators throughout business, media and political circles: 'Shall we park that one for now?' says the person who wants to avoid either having their own idea rejected or making a decision on somebody else's idea.

Usually, it's a dishonest way of saying 'no', a bit like saying, 'Let's put it on the back burner for now,' or 'Interesting. Let's talk about that later.' Among commissioning editors at television networks there are hundreds of different weaselly ways of saying 'no' to a pitch for a programme, most of which translate as 'we've got thousands of ideas we don't want, can't you just leave us alone?' As this is the truth, these excuses are forgivable, but what makes 'park' worse is the casual nature in which it is expressed; the suggestion that, 'of course, we'll come back to it later'. But they never come back to it. The idea is left in an exposed corner on a baking-hot day until it slowly suffocates like a dog in the back seat of a car.

Fauxmance

'Fauxmance' circulates in the same watering holes as those other nauseating words 'frenemy' and 'chillax' and again it reflects as badly on the user as it does on the people it describes. A 'fauxmance' is a faux romance between two celebrities who aren't really shagging each other but pretend they are because the publicity is good for both of them. Various dismal fake couplings have been concocted over recent years – Geri Haliwell and Chris Evans, Kerry Katona and Peter Andre, Madonna and some bloke called Jesus, Cheryl Cole and some bloke from the Black Eyed Peas, Jennifer Aniston and … well, just some blokes. There are, sadly, dozens more couples I could list, but it would be pointless as I've no idea who they are.

Yes, 'fauxmancing' is a blatant manipulation of the media by celebrities with no apparent concern for their various relatives and exes and children, but it's actually more like a partnership. Because just like the paparazzi photographer who splits the money he gets for his exclusive shot of (let's call her) Starlet X leaving Le Tosser's nightclub, as it was she who tipped him off she was going to Le Tosser's in the first place, so the tabloids and the gossip mags sell thousands more copies by covering the contrived smooches of the fake coupling and probably a few more copies by 'exposing' the deception as if the notion of celebrities not being what they seem was somehow news. And the horrible smugness and self-satisfaction of the synthesised word 'fauxmance' sums up the whole business perfectly. So anyone using it to describe this sort of tawdry behaviour secretly can't get enough of it.

Which sadly leads us on to …

Bromance

Like many of the words I really hate, 'bromance' belongs in the group of made-up words called 'portmanteau'; this was coined by Lewis Carroll to describe the words he created in *Through the*

Looking Glass, including for example the combination of chuckle and snort – 'chortle'. Despite my dislike of the portmanteau concept, I really like 'chortle', it sounds as old as it is, and it adds colour to the language. Another top portmanteau word is 'gerrymandering', which describes the dodgy tactics of Massachusetts's governor Elbridge Thomas Gerry in redrawing electoral boundaries in 1812 to benefit himself, leaving the demarcation lines twisting and turning like a salamander. It's a stroke of literary genius and feels almost onomatopoeic. These words create something new or explain something quite complicated and have stood the test of time in a way that 'bromance' shouldn't and, with any luck, won't. 'Bromance' is used to describe a close male relationship without any sexual attraction, although that's what normal people would call a 'friendship'. The term is commonly used in ghastly celebrity gossip rags and tabloids to describe two famous men, usually film stars, who spend a lot of time in each other's company. These media organs will shrivel up and die if they can't write about who's shagging who, so, faced with the prospect of a couple of attractive men not shagging anyone, male or female, or each other, they have to describe them in a way that suggests *something* is going on, so they go for 'bromance'.

And they have the editor of a skateboard magazine to thank for coining the term in the 1990s to describe the relationship between two platonic skateboarders who spent a lot of time together. Surprisingly, the terms 'Ollie', 'Nollie', 'Fakie' and 'Nosegrind' never made it into popular usage but a description of two ordinary blokes just minding their own business and concentrating on not falling off their stupid tea tray on wheels did survive and is now beginning to contaminate every aspect of our culture, some of which was established years before the word was even thought of.

Apparently, Sherlock Holmes and Dr Watson displayed early 'bromantic' tendencies; that's according to the quality film-maker and respected literary critic Guy Ritchie. So constant companions who respect and love each other cannot be allowed to be just that. No, they have to be having a 'bromance'. And all those great partnerships we've enjoyed on film and TV over the decades, like Butch Cassidy and the Sundance Kid, Rick Blaine and Captain Renault, Starsky and Hutch, Regan and Carter in *The Sweeney*, Freebie and the Bean, Bob Hope and Bing Crosby, Abbot and Costello, Laurel and Hardy, Morecambe and Wise, they weren't friendships at all … they were actually 'bromances'.

This is plainly the biggest skip-load of nonsense since author Kevin Sandler's analysis* of Bugs Bunny cartoons in which he claimed, 'Bugs' transvestism reinforces the alignment of gender, sex and sexuality ideals by denaturalising and defamiliarising them through gender transgression'. As Bugs might say: 'What a maroon'.

Reading the Rabbit: Explorations in Warner Bros. Animation by Kevin Sandler

BFF

A 'BF' is not, as you might expect, a Bloody Fool; it's a Best Friend. A 'BFF' is a Best Friend Forever, despite the strong likelihood that anyone who confines the expression of their friendship to initials doesn't deserve to be friends with anyone for long.

It's a curious fact about the present Information Age (if that's what we are still calling it; I'm a bit out of touch) that the ludicrous ease with which people can accumulate 'friends' has stretched the definition of the word until it's saggier than the elastic on Eamonn Holmes's Y-fronts.

I asked around some young people in my office whether a Facebook friend is firmer than a 'BFF'. The howls of derision told me that it's a bit of a cliché for old people like me to bemoan the sincerity of Facebook friends, but what is anyone to make of the notion of a 'BFF' when celebrity websites and magazines attribute a close relationship to people who just happen to be photographed together?

Here are some examples of photo captions from some recently papped celebrities (we can't afford to show the actual photos):

'Heidi Klum and Gwen Stefani are not a likely pair but their
families like to hang out'
(They are standing awkwardly in the road)

'Kristen Stewart and Dakota Fanning have seen quite
a bit of each other in the last year'
(Whoever they are, they seem to have been in the same film)

'Jessica Simpson is joined at the hip to her stylist Ken Paves'
(He works for her)

After reeling at the notion that anyone called Ken Paves would feature in celebrity gossip, and genuinely not having a clue who these people are, I decided to do a bit of research (three clicks, actually) and I discovered that being seen around with a 'stylist' if you are a famous person is not at all unusual, but fair enough if you really like each other. Uh-oh, though, what's this on *E! News*?

They've had a major fight. Ken recently tweeted a shoutout for his friends,
but didn't include Jessica in that list.

No! What a bastard.

So they are not 'BFFs' any more, although by the time you read this bit they may well be back 'on' again, just like a couple of teenage girls. Which is exactly the root of my problem with 'BFF'. It's a teenage girl's phrase that has been adopted generally by older women, who perhaps use it partly ironically but deep down think it might help them stave off growing old – the verbal equivalent of a good pair of skinny jeans.

Staycation

All the reasons for writing this book are contained within this single, hideous Frankenstein of a word. There's the smugness that lies behind all the other portmanteau words out there ('frenemy', 'bromance', 'chillax', etc.) combined with the ugliness of one of the worst Americanisms – 'vacation', which no one ever uses in this country – plus the marketing manure its usage scatters onto the travel industry.

The more popular term in Britain for the stay-at-home holiday is a 'stoliday' or a 'holistay', according to Wikipedia, which has excelled itself with this particular made-up fact, as it involves two totally made-up, nonexistent words. Sadly, although no one in Britain has ever, or will ever use 'stoliday' or 'holistay', an alarming number of people do use 'staycation'. No sooner did the word begin to circulate in a few twattish travel supplements than dozens of other travel hacks took it up and now there are companies called Staycation.org offering the antidote to holidays abroad.

Why can't people say that they either simply can't afford or simply can't be bothered to go abroad? Instead, they concoct all sorts of bogus reasons for choosing to holiday at home, dredging up all that old bollocks about children doing what 'we' always used to do on Enid Blyton-style holidays in the past, such as pond-dipping (catching slime in a net), ducks and drakes (throwing stones), crabbing (falling off rocks) and lighting a beach bonfire (vandalism). And for a holiday that is supposed to be based on 'staying put', a staycation seems to involve an awful lot of charging about visiting those 'local attractions we take for granted the rest of the year'.

There is something infuriating about the need for journalists and holidaymakers to describe a British holiday in this way. I have banged on at great length elsewhere (*Can't Be Arsed*, £9.99) about the folly of foreign travel and the beauty of staying put; no one needs to be ashamed of holidaying in Britain, but the people who use 'staycation' are exactly those who would still snorkel in the Maldives if they could afford it. Like millions of others in the last ten years, they have lived beyond their means and a word like 'staycation' makes them feel less like they've fallen on hard times, especially if they got it from the *Telegraph* travel supplement.

Fit for Purpose

This ugly phrase comes from the murky world of Quality Assurance. I don't want to dwell on 'QA' for too long, mainly because I've no idea what it is, and that's exactly how its practitioners like it. The less we know about Quality Assurance, Total Networking Solutions, Modality Management, International Logistics, Systems Analysis and the like, the more they can charge us for it. Basically, it's something like management consultancy. Some people have a look at what's happening inside an organisation and say whether it's working efficiently or not. Then they walk off with all the money in fees that might have helped make the organisation work efficiently.

Translated into proper English, 'fit for purpose' means 'does what it's supposed to do'. For example, the editorial department of Quality Book Publishing Limited is supposed to make happen for words what I write in this book are good and the right number of them to cost for £9.99. If it can't manage that, then the boss of Quality Books would probably say that the editorial department is rubbish.* However, a management consultant might say 'the editorial department is not fit for purpose', because, of course, no one would have the cheek to

*which of course it ain't.

charge £100,000 in consultancy fees just for saying something's rubbish. But a phrase like 'not fit for purpose' implies there's a mutual understanding of what an organisation's purpose is – 'we've really got to grips with your business and we know what you're trying to achieve'. Although what most organisations are trying to achieve is staying afloat and paying people at the end of the month.

So 'fit for purpose' means OK and not 'fit for purpose' means useless. However, it's also a phrase which ambitious politicians and civil servants are reaching for more and more when they want subtly to stick the boot in to prison officers or immigration officials or teachers or social workers or anyone else they can dump on to their own advantage. If an ingenious prisoner escapes from jail or a cunning asylum seeker slips through the net or a vicious, illiterate monster kicks his girlfriend's child to death, the ambitious politician, rather than credit or condemn the individual actually responsible for the action, will blame the organisation which allowed it to happen. He'll say the Prison Inspectorate/Home Office/Social Services Department of Hackney Council is not 'fit for purpose'. By using this sort of buzzword bollocks, he signals to the people in the know – the journalists and spin doctors and other people who can assist his promotion – that he has a grasp of management and an understanding of 'structures', while at the same time not resorting to anything so uncouth as blaming individuals. Eventually, an inquiry can be set up, probably employing some highly expensive management consultants, to *prove* that the organisation is not 'fit for purpose' and then various individual social workers or prison officers can be scapegoated in the newspapers and sacked.

Best Practice

Another phrase from the Management Consultant's Bumper Book of Buzzword Bollocks, 'best practice' is the kind of phrase you will hear trotted out by local government officers, chairmen of hospital trusts and cabinet ministers after some bungling by a department or organisation which has been labelled not 'fit for purpose'. They will promise something like a 'root and branch reorganisation involving a widespread retraining programme in line with best practice'.

Many people are clearly convinced 'best practice' is meaningful and important because several organisations seem to exist to promote it or charge for it, e.g. SharepointBestpractices.co.uk. Here's what they say they do:

Best Practices is about the most efficient, effective ways to achieve goals, distilled into adaptable, repeatable procedures you can use; the Core Methods that achieve the best outcomes – giving you a framework to break the cycle of avoidance, disagreement and subpar results and leverage the hard-won experience of industry leaders.

Does that actually mean anything? How about this from bestpractice.uk.com?

Best Practice Training & Development is the UK's leading provider of skills training and vocational qualifications for customer service, contact centre, business support, leadership and management.

Nope, still none the wiser. Perhaps the Best Practice Club can shed some light on it?

It's vital that organisations retain their customers and effective complaint resolution/service recovery is a constituent part of any robust customer management strategy. In these interesting times how do you deal effectively with service recovery challenges?

So let's get this straight – they offer businesses training and advice on how to train and advise their customer service advisers on how to explain to customers what businesses do.

The confusion you're probably experiencing now is probably what the best-practitioners want. More and more middle managers are using 'best practice' to give the impression that their work is quantifiable; that they know exactly what they are doing and that somehow the totally nebulous meaningless paper/email-pushing departments and Titanic Deckchair Realignment Solutions-type companies have a genuine, useful purpose which can be measured.

Let's say 'best practice' is another, far more annoying way of saying 'doing your job properly' or a good idea about how to change the way you do your job. The assumption that a particular way of doing a job should be tested and codified and laid down in a rulebook so that everyone in an organisation can do things the same way is ludicrous and stupid and offends against common sense. It explains why call-centre operatives work from scripts so dull you could be listening to *The Archers* and why most customer service people dealing with your complaint 'can only apologise'. We all owe it to each other to reject 'best practice', embrace the slapdash and do our respective jobs as badly as possible.

Vagazzle

It's a measure of how low we have sunk as a civilisation that, of all the different ways to spell this combination of vagina and dazzle, 90 per cent of the occurrences of it on Google are wrong. You get vejazzle, vajazzle, vajazle, vegazzle (do they think it is part vegetable?) but very rarely, 'vagazzle'. None of the millions of poltroons around the English-speaking world for whom this word has opened up new opportunities to parade their trashiness seems to know that vagina is spelled with a 'g'.

It's an even more significant measure of how low we have sunk that the mere combination of two such words to form another is sufficient for thousands of stupid people to act upon it. It has echoes of 'If you build it, they will come' – 'If you name it, they will stick sequins on it'.

It's all thanks to Jennifer Love Hewitt, a Hollywood actress/singer who may well have various talents but gives the appearance of being so vacuous that she could exert the gravitational pull of a black hole. She was appearing on a chat show hosted by tiny, moustachioed Latino freak George Lopez on American TV (if you thought the audience on *10 O'Clock Live* were moronic, just listen to the nutters whooping on this show), when she began to describe how she felt a bit low one night after the tabloids had written about her sex life. You have to understand that Jennifer Love Hewitt has slept with most of the men in Hollywood, so the chances are that, if it was tabloid coverage she was upset about, she could have been describing any night of the year. Anyway, to cheer herself up, she did what anyone would do and asked her mate to 'come over with some Swarovski crystals and vagazzle my special lady'. Heeeurrrg! Retch! The way some people describe their own genitals is often more nauseating than if they showed you a blown-up photograph of them.

So what does this 'vagazzling' entail? Basically sticking some shiny objects around the shaved fanny area. It seems that some women have become so bored with arse tattoos and extreme genital topiary that, like a junkie who has run out of veins and begins injecting into his eyeball, they have turned to a more serious level of self-mutilation. It's as if their own bodies were so repellent that they would rather they themselves were plastic figurines: 'vagazzling' is the sort of thing a bored child would do to a Barbie doll. The Huffington Post website called the vagazzle 'a merkin for 21st-century airheads', and indeed it does remind

remind me of an actor preparing to play a part which requires a particularly mad wig. First they shave their heads, then apply the bald wig, then the main wig on top. Similarly, the 'vagazzling' girl first makes herself bald and then applies a sequinned wig to play the part of a total fuckwit.

So, the great guru Jennifer Love Hewitt coins a ridiculous term on television and, because the combination of words is appealing to the imbeciles in Hollywood and the lame-brained sheep who follow their doings, 'vagazzling' spreads like the clap. Again, because it's America it's almost understandable; their mental processes have been severely impaired by some kind of brain-shrivelling virus for half a century. Unfortunately, this virus arrived in Britain about fifteen years ago (via Jerry Springer probably) and is widespread among particularly vulnerable communities in the Southeast, like Buckhurst Hill and Chigwell, where some of the people are now so stupid they would lobotomise themselves if you could come up with a good enough word for it.

Thanks to the terrifying reality/soap *The Only Way Is Essex*, the word 'vagazzle' is being casually passed around, as if it were a standard beauty-therapy like a facial or pedicure, among the chattering classes who like to think of themselves as superior to people from Chigwell but who will soon, mark my words, find themselves 'vagazzling', just because it's the latest thing to do. It's as if you were to walk into a barber's and the price list on the wall included haircut/blow dry/shave/Prince Albert/butt plug.

96

LOL

● ●

If someone tells a good joke you can laugh at it, and if someone tells a stinker you can say it's rubbish or just boo. But if you can't see the person telling you the joke, how do you let them know that you liked it? And if you're the teller of the joke, how do you know if your efforts have been appreciated? Can you imagine how awful it must have been for those early pioneers of talking-shit-to-each-other-via-a-computer-screen-or-texting-keypad, as they sent their half-baked observations and poorly formed sentences out into the ether, never knowing if the recipient so much as cracked a smile at 'c u l8er 2day 4 6'. In the old days when kids were writing '8OO8S' or 'SHI7' on calculators, they were rewarded by the visible and audible amusement of their friends as well as very poor maths results, but for this screen-fixated, self-obsessed, digital generation the lack of feedback was a problem as intractable as the search for longitude or the cure for syphilis. But then some genius, we will never know who, came up with 'LOL' – Laughing Out Loud.* It's the perfect response for both the sender and the recipient, and it obeys the First Commandment of the digital doctrine that, whatever you

---

*Even I know it's not 'Lots Of Love'.

do, it should take up as little time, effort, money and characters as possible. It's probably the most popular text abbreviation along with 'OMG' and 'BF' and has broken out of the texting enclosure to begin breeding with normal language, to the point where some linguists are crediting digital language and textspeak with the same influence and impact on our culture as Latin and Greek. *Tanti coleones!*

I can appreciate that there's ingenuity in the way some text language has been developed – 'w8' meaning wait, for example, or 'A3' meaning any time, any place, anywhere and, my particular favourite, '@:-}' meaning a smiling Sikh. But these clever codes are no more a language and a culture than an extended game of Dingbats.

Other linguists admire the brevity and range of expression in textspeak but compare the elegance of Orwell or Hemingway's stripped-down language with 'ROFLMAO' (Rolling on floor laughing my arse off). As for the range of expression, it boils down simply to 'Like' and 'Dislike'. Someone posts a video of themselves on YouTube, falling off a trampoline or getting their head stuck in a basketball hoop, and the response is either a thumb up or a thumb down; either 'LOL' or 'FAIL' (see p. 127).

There is another big problem with 'LOL', and the reason why it belongs in this book. Because, as I said in the introduction, I don't have a problem with young people using their own slang, it's the inappropriate use of that slang by grown-ups or the fundamental dishonesty of a particular phrase which warrants its inclusion in this list. And 'LOL' is dishonest because it's almost exclusively used nowadays by people who are not laughing out loud. They are pretending to do so to be amusingly ironic (can you have an ironic acronym?) or out of politeness, which is a terrifically old-fashioned way of using such a 21st-century phrase. Someone whose feelings you don't want to hurt sends you a text joke which you think is a bit shit, but all you have to do is send 'LOL'. They get the pat on the head they are after and you can tell yourself you haven't lied to them because you've been ironic. It can be as insincere as the polite laughter of a Regency drawing room. It's remarkable that three little letters that mean so little seem on the verge of taking over the world.

Bandwidth

• •

'Bandwidth' is another one of those undesirably alien, techie terms which has arrived clinging to the undercarriage of the IT mumbo-jumbo as it lands squarely in the runway of everyday speech. Like 'let's take this offline' (talk about it later) and 'ping' (send), it's beginning to be heard more and more outside the confines of software development companies. Someone I know claims they hear these terms in what they call 'scrum standups'. These are basically gatherings of people having a meeting in an office, who have no doubt been summoned by a senior person clapping their hands and shouting, 'Listen up, people' (see p. 115).

'Bandwidth' is a self-consciously complicated way of saying something simple and straightforward; the complete arse's attempt to say he's too busy to take on extra work. Not too lazy, you understand, but too busy. Of course, plain old 'busy' won't do because it suggests that he can't cope with his own workload, whereas 'insufficient bandwidth' suggests it's someone else's problem and in that sense it's similar to the rather childish 'it's above my paygrade' excuse – 'I would have played with you but you didn't ask me nicely'.

Blaming it on the 'bandwidth' (as opposed to the sunshine, moonlight or boogie) means 'I simply don't have the capacity to accommodate your request'. Yes if only those bastards upstairs had cabled you up properly, you'd have helped out willingly. Let's put to one side the fact that in most cases people who claim they are too busy to help are lying (no one who works in an office can ever really have too much work on) and let's not mention the old proverb about bad workmen blaming their tools, but let's ask instead whether anyone with an ounce of self-respect would ever want to compare their ability to do something to the length or thickness of a piece of wire.

98

Deliverables

● ●

Yet more business bollocks; a 'deliverable' is a twat's word for whatever you are supposed to achieve in your job. As far as this book is concerned, about 250 pages of printed writing and a colourful picture on the front cover was my editor's 'deliverable'; the actual writing of it was mine. Of course, neither of us would have used the word at any stage of the process or we would probably have stabbed each other to death.

The spread of the word 'deliverables' is a consequence of the cranking up of the word 'deliver' by cock-waving, macho businessmen into something cool and powerful. 'There, see. I delivered. Promised it. Delivered it. Job Done.' ('Deliver' is never far from 'job done'.) Equally, an inability to 'deliver' is the ultimate sign of weakness. 'Yeah, couldn't hack it. Didn't deliver.' Not 'delivering' is the sort of thing Gordon Ramsay would accuse the trembling chef of a country pub of on *Kitchen Nightmares*, if the evening's service fell apart. 'You didn't deliver. Where are your bollocks?' It's remarkable that a word meant to describe something as straightforward (and useful) as turning up with a cardboard box in a van and leaving it on a customer's doorstep has become so butch and manly.

'Deliverables' is another way of saying 'target' and it's no surprise that it really took hold in the tieless, sleeves-up, footyloving, beer-swilling, sofa-lounging Lord Protectorate of Alastair Campbell. There was nothing New Labour loved more than behaving like the bankers and billionaire businessmen who marched to power with them and who proceeded to get even richer at the future's expense. Tony, Gordon, Peter and Alastair would prove to the world that they could run public services properly, in a businesslike way, and barely had the furniture vans begun to unload at Number 10 than the policy wonks and unelected back-room puppetmeisters were sitting down with the politicians to devise 'business plans' and set targets for every walk of public life from policing to the NHS to teaching. Then they had to waste millions more man-hours devising ways to measure these targets and efficiency goals and came up with ridiculous, businesslike words to describe what they were doing, such as 'stakeholder' and, of course, 'deliverables'. Suddenly it became socially acceptable to talk like a management consultant in the operating theatre as well as the office. If it was OK for the NHS, then it was OK for you. The legacy of those early Blairite days can be seen in the kind of guff you can find on 'how to manage' websites all over the internet:

Internal deliverables are the outputs of the project tasks that serve as inputs to other project tasks. The external deliverables serve as inputs to making the stakeholder's deliverables complete.

Politicians should inspire us, not suffocate us in a fug of tedious jargon. Can you imagine Winston Churchill in 1940 saying 'Never in the field of human conflict were so many deliverables outputted to stakeholders with such limited human resources'?

● ● ●

It's hard to believe that three tiny punctuation marks could be in any way offensive but, just as there are no bounds to the ingenuity of mankind when it comes to devising methods of torture, so there are no limits on the crimes that total arseholes can perpetrate against the English language.

And, while many truly horrible tortures have been devised in the name of religion or a particular ideology, these punctuation marks have been twisted and corrupted in the name of a far more harmful and destructive cause – hype.

Now I don't mean offensive punctuation in the Lynne Truss/Grammar Nazi way; or the three dots that are used a lot in 'humorous' writing to suggest some amusing consequences which we can – tee-hee – only imagine (an abbreviated version of 'let's not go there!'). I'm talking about three full stops, harmless in themselves, but, in the wrong combination, highly inflammatory. I'm afraid, in the interests of greater understanding, I will have to lay them out for you now in the offending manner:

Oh. My. God.

Do you recognise them now? They quickly moved on from here when the phrase mutated into the more powerful OMG

(see p. 15)
but now they are more commonly found in:

Best. Movie. Ever.

(*See also*: Best. Gig. Ever. Fastest. Car. Ever. Funniest. YouTube. Ever. Hottest. Babe. Ever.)

You should see the grammar and spellcheck underscores on the Word programme as I type these hideous phrases. I had to override the autocorrect function *five times* before I could press on with a sentence; the poor comma is so disorientated it must think it is adrift in a Year 1 Literacy exercise book. But it's not just the crimes against grammar and punctuation which offend, it's the idea that it's possible to convince someone of a claim that is already absurd (is *The Last Airbender in 3D* really the Best. Movie. Ever?) by expressing it in the form of a shitty film trailer with a voiceover from that bloke who does all of them; the kind which begins 'In a world where ... [INSERT BOLLOCKS] ... One man is [MORE NONSENSE] and ends with [INSERT STUPID TITLE AND OVERBLOWN MEANINGLESS STRAPLINE E.G.] ... The firing. Stops. When the stopping. Fires.'

Do. These morons. Think. That I. Have Such. A Short Attention Span. That I can only process. One. Word. At. A. Time?

Needless to say, the three evil dots – which were spawned in America to the disgust, I should add, of many right-thinking Americans – are arriving in this country like bubonic fleas on the backs of rats; the rats being, er, internet things in my rather convoluted simile. Not convinced? Consider this: there is an App for your smartphone called Best. Night. Ever. It's like a more toxic and contagious version of Facebook through which, if you're not familiar with it, people can send each other photos of themselves and their mates gurning and sticking their tongues out. No sound is audible but you can imagine them all going 'woooooo!'

Anyway, this App lets you rank your best nights ever – where you were, what you did, who you puked on – and add to each entry the photos and quotes from people on the night. There's bound to be one entry from someone's mate, no doubt called Chris, saying something totally random and someone else literally laughing their ass off – OMG he's genius!

The promotional blurb for the App suggests you can, from time to time, look at your archive of Best. Nights. Ever. and reminisce. Amazing. I don't know how we got by for the last couple of millennia without such a thing, except perhaps by putting things in a 'diary' – that radical technical innovation that allowed you to record your Best. Nights. Ever. in a book, so that you could easily bring your memories to life again by reading them. Unfortunately, the diary demands of the user two skills which the digital age is rapidly rendering obsolete. Reading. And. Writing.

Literally

Quite literally the most overused and incorrectly applied word in the English language,

When people say 'literally', they usually mean figuratively or metaphorically. If someone says 'I was literally spitting feathers', it means they were actually spitting feathers. Which, of course, they weren't. Unless they had accidentally burst open a pillow, inhaled some feathers and, rather than using language figuratively to create a picture of a very thirsty person whose mouth feels like it is full of feathers,* they were using the expression to describe what actually happened.

But who cares about the difference between literally and figuratively?

Most people just use literally as an intensifier, like really or absolutely, don't they?

These are questions frequently asked by literally no one (apart from me just now) because regular abusers of the word 'literally'

---

*This is the original meaning of the phrase; the 'angry' sense stems from a 1970s malapropism.

don't give a damn about proper English. The fact is, people have been literally-ing to the annoyance or amusement of grammarians for over 100 years and *Private Eye*'s Colemanballs would be so much the poorer without it – 'Terry Venables has literally had his legs cut off from underneath him three times while he's been manager' is my particular favourite.

But there has been a more alarming development in recent years: Young People have imported it into the increasingly influential Facebook/YouTube/text-speak, slap-each-other-on-the-back lexicon of digital insincerity. Look at this genuine comment from a scary YouTube video:

You will literally say 'Oh My God' while watching it.

Or this comment on an 'amusing' blog photo

Lol wtf!? Literally laughed my ass off.

You will find literally thousands of instances of literally in the same 'sentence' as 'Oh My God' and 'laugh my ass off'. Admittedly, I got lucky with one that contained literally, LOL *and* WTF as well, but take a good look at the use of the word 'literally' in that sentence. It's a given that no one is laughing out loud when they use LOL (see p. 207) but we also know that they are definitely not parting company with their 'ass' either. So the use of the word 'literally' is actually strengthening the lack of factual accuracy; it's a *reverse intensifier* if that's possible.

'Literally' is now so embedded in cool tweeny/teen/ Facebooky language that if you were a student you would hear it literally a hundred times a day. And, as we can see in all walks of life, adults are becoming more and more like children with every passing year, either by copying youthful behaviour or simply refusing to grow up, so that talking like teenagers and students has become just as much a part of this Peter Pan syndrome as 'girly nights in' and 'boys' weekends'.

Given that it's almost impossible to halt the spread of the abusive form of 'literally' (the grammatical argument for not using it will only spur people on), we will have to adjust our understanding of the term and accept, nay actively encourage, the spread of a new definition of the word 'literally': 'not true'.

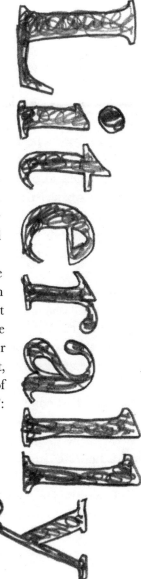

101

End Of

• •

There ought to be a physical movement that goes along with 'end of' whenever it is used in conversation, and at least a full stop every time it is written down, but I imagine that would never survive the impatience of anyone who actually uses it. Five years ago, idiots might have said, 'Talk to the hand 'cos the face ain't listening' – along with a hand shoved angrily in your face – quite witty in its own way, but so much of our language now is subject to fashion that only a plonker (is that right?) would say that these days.

I don't have any objection to people telling me when they've stopped talking, because walking off before they've finished could be seen as rude. Perhaps they could just try saying 'over' like disaster-bound pilots do in war films or action movies. Or, as they used to do in American TV shows, 'period'. That never really caught on over here, for a fairly obvious reason: 'No, I'm fine. I don't want to talk about it. I'm not in a bad mood. Period.'

The real tragedy with 'end of' is that middle-aged and elderly men across the country have started saying it, usually a few milliseconds before saying the cringeworthy 'job done'. An utterly horrific example of this occurred recently at the

Conservative Party Conference when Tim Loughton, a Junior Minister for Twattery, I assume, said it four times in response to questions from a journalist about government policy. The poor fool's pomposity was inversely proportional to how cool he thought he was. In his head, he thought he was saying:

'I haven't time for you, I'm busy – I have my crack whores to collect from then I'll get in my ride back to my crib in East Worthing and Shoreham.'

We probably shouldn't be surprised that our very own cussin' Prime Minister David Cameron uses 'end of'. When Labour were in power and the Lockerbie bomber was released, he told reporters: 'Al Megrahi should have completed his sentence – end of.'

One day, David Cameron will finish Prime Minister's Questions with 'Laters'.

If you check your *Nostradamus*, you'll find that the use of 'end of' by posh old Tories is one of the harbingers of the apocalypse and you'll really know that the Last Judgement is on its way the day after Ann Widdecombe starts saying it.

At the end of the 1956 classic film *High Society*, Louis Armstrong is playing opposite Frank Sinatra, Bing Crosby and Grace Kelly and he's still the coolest person there. It's the end of a film, literally the end of the story and he says, 'End of story'. He doesn't say 'end of'; he's not concerned with the millisecond he saves by dropping the word 'story' because he knows, what seemingly everyone else doesn't, that it is not cool to say 'end of'.

All of the words and phrases in this book should be avoided like the plague but some can become even more objectionable depending on which sex uses them. Here's a handy guide:

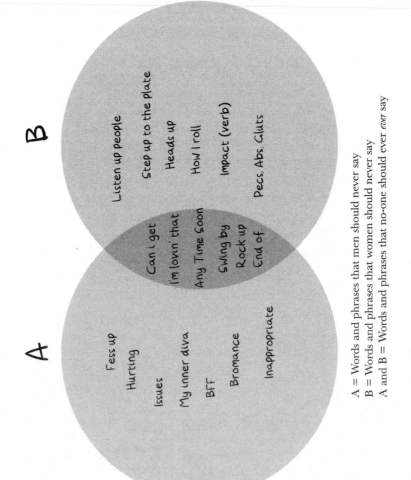

B

Listen up people

Step up to the plate

Heads up

How I roll

Impact (verb)

Pecs, Abs, Gluts

Can I get

I'm lovin' that

Any Time Soon

Swing by

Rock up

End of.

A

Fess up

Hurting

Issues

My inner diva

BFF

Bromance

Inappropriate

A = Words and phrases that men should never say
B = Words and phrases that women should never say
A and B = Words and phrases that no-one should *ever ever* say

ACKNOWLEDGEMENTS

●●●

First and foremost thanks to my wife Stephanie for the idea for the book, several of the entries and, after much discussion, the title (not, as you might think, based on 20 years of listening to me).

Thanks also to my agent, Jennifer Christie, for negotiating the generous delivery deadline for the manuscript, which I then managed to miss; and to my editor Malcolm for his patience, sensible suggestions and determination to confront my over-reliance of the hyphen – although it can be useful sometimes.

Also thanks to the following for their suggestions for words and phrases to include, some of which I didn't use this time but which I have stored in my head so that I can get annoyed whenever I hear people using them:

Helen Arnold, Mark Barrett, Neil Christie, Jon Davenport, Peter Dean, Jonathan Harvey, Monica Long, Suj Summer and Mark Wilson.

RICHARD WILSON

CAN'T BE ARSED

101 THINGS NOT TO DO
BEFORE YOU DIE

"I'd like to say that this is a funny, intelligent, thorough account of
not bothering to expand your horizons, but I can't be arsed."
Paul Merton

Here's a fact: there are at least 100 books out there that tell you
the various things you should do before you die. (There may be
more but we couldn't be arsed to count them.) 'Swim with
dolphins!' – they squeal. Jump out of a plane from a great
height! Read Kafka in Prague! Have a meaningful conversation
with a beggar! (Yes, really.)

But will these things actually make our lives more meaningful?

For those who are looking for an escape-route; a guilt-free reason
NOT to spend their hard-earned cash on deli-belly in India, or
broken limbs on the ski slopes of the Alps, Can't Be Arsed shows
the other side of the coin. It hilariously exposes the harsh reality
of these so-called 'adventures', giving you the perfect excuse to
stay at home and crack open a beer on the sofa.

£9.99 • Hardback • 9781906032371